Also by Saylor Storm
Dr. Selfish

"Flattery words are but honey coated poison."

Saylor Storm

With Malicious Intent

Mully,
In appreciation.
Saylor Storm

With Malicious Intent is a work of fiction. Names, characters, places and incidents are either a product of the author's imagination or are used fictitiously. Any resemblance to actual persons, living or dead, events or locals is entirely coincidental unless you are suffering from delusions of grandeur.

Originally published on my ink jet printer for my editor to tear apart.

Cover design by John Phelan

Dedication

To my dear friends who have been there long before the conception of the Saylor Storm novels and who have participated with enthusiasm, loving support and hard work.

Katherine Bourne

Darlene Fairbank

Grace Gore

Linda McCall

Lora McKay (Phil)

Kathy Potnick

Steven Roberts

Michael Stocking

Chapter 1

Zachary Taylor's milk was poisoned during an Independence Day celebration.

"I'm sorry, Mr. Graham, there's nothing more that can be done." The nurse spoke quickly wanting to end the awkward conversation as soon as possible.

Robert's suffering face was pale as he looked at the ground while she spoke. He looked intensely into her eyes. "Please, nurse, there must be something left to try. We can't leave these four children without a mother."

They both glanced across the room to the four children huddled in the corner of the hospital room.

Robert's eyes swelled with tears as he spoke. "Please, I beg of you. We have to try something! We can't just give up!"

The nurse repeated herself. "I'm sorry Mr. Graham, there's nothing more to try."

Robert tried to compose himself for his children's sake. They looked at their father with anticipation and dread. They feared that he was about to deliver some bad news about their mother...the worst. "Nurse, will you please take my children out into the hallway, so I can say goodbye to my wife in private."

"Of course, Mr. Graham." She quickly escorted the four children out of the room.

Robert pulled a chair up to Hannah's bedside. Even in his distraught state, Robert was a handsome man. A full head of rich brown hair, parted on the side and big brown eyes that told all that he was feeling. At six feet he looked like a vulnerable child, his lower lip quivering as he spoke slowly to Hannah.

He took her small pale hand in both of his, playing with the two rings on her left hand. "Hannah, I love you more than anything in this world. I beg of you, please don't leave me. Please don't leave our children. We all love you and need you. We'll be lost without you!" He hung his head and wept. There was no reaction from Hannah.

Robert composed himself enough to speak again. "Hannah, if you must go, just know how much you mean to me, always have and always will. My life would have been nothing without you." He buried his head in her lap sobbing uncontrollably.

The pale figure was scarcely visible against the white hospital sheets. In recent weeks, her once vibrant frame had withered away to nearly half her former size. Hannah did not move, not even to open her eyes.

Robert composed himself. He stood up, leaned over Hannah and kissed her on the forehead, all the while holding her left hand in both of his.

He walked into the hallway, huddling quietly with his children. "Kids, I know this is very difficult for you, but your mother is dying. Would any of you like to say goodbye to her? It's okay if you don't. Your mother will understand."

The tears were flowing freely; Robert put his arms around them. Ten-year-old Charley spoke first, "Yes, Dad, I would like to say goodbye to Mom."

Robert asked the nurse to stay with the girls while he escorted Charley inside. Charley was a miniature version of his dad, soft brown hair, big expressive brown eyes; he even wore the same polo shirts that his father always wore.

Charley broke down the moment he saw his mother, he ran to her bedside and threw his arms around her frail body. "Mommy please don't die! Mommy, please don't go!"

Robert watched his son from the doorway, trying his best to control his emotions. He felt like losing it completely and joining his son in an emotional release. He let Charley have his time alone with her and then escorted him back to the hallway. Charley was crying out of control. Robert just held him.

"Would you girls like to say goodbye to Mommy, too?" All three nodded as they cried. Robert led them to Hannah's bedside. The three huddled together not knowing what to do or say. Val at eight looked like a young woman, thin build, long dark blond hair and the round Graham brown eyes. Her sister Alexa at six though very similar, had more of an athletic build. Little Ginny at three had the same coloring as her sisters, but was very much still the baby. The three stood huddle next to their mother's bedside, just sobbing.

Robert brought Charley back into the room. As the family waited numbly for Hannah's impending death, a team of doctors arrived at her hospital room door, all bearing wide smiles. They introduced themselves as visiting specialists from University of Kansas. Robert could not help notice how their smiling faces looked out of place.

"We have news," one of the doctors announced to Robert. "We have pinpointed the source of your wife's illness and we have a cure."

The news took a moment to settle in to Robert's confused brain. "What are you telling me?" Robert wanted to know. "You mean my wife is going to be okay?"

"Yes," the doctor replied. "There will be some temporary damage to her internal organs, but that will pass in a few weeks. She should be nearly fully recovered in a matter of days."

Robert began to weep. All four children stared at their father in confusion.

The still smiling doctor started to explain, "Your wife had been poisoned, as far as we can tell, off and on for many, many weeks."

Robert listened, speechless, in shock.

"We've located the poison and have added B12 and insulin to her IV. Her organs should respond very nicely."

"I don't understand," Robert muttered. "Who would want to poison Hannah?"

"That," the doctor said, "we don't know. You will have to find that out on your own."

The team of doctors left the room just as quickly as they had entered. Robert grabbed his children and hugged them tightly as they all wept openly.

Chapter 2

Napoleon Bonaparte killed someone on his staff with arsenic.

A dozen years earlier, Hannah Ellsworth had been a spunky freshman at Georgetown University. She had a fresh-scrubbed quality about her. She was the girl that all of the other girls wanted to hate, but couldn't. A perfect scholar, a formidable athlete and just plain nice, she appeared to have it all. At 5'5" her athletic frame suited her sports of choice: soccer and track. Her golden blond hair lay straight, landing somewhere mid back. Her round, dark brown eyes were striking against the contrast of her light hair. She was an unpretentious, natural beauty.

Hannah moved into her first dorm room her freshman year at Georgetown with her sorority sister, Lori. The two appeared to have little in common. Lori was shy, dark, overweight and non-athletic. Lori was surprised that someone like Hannah would give her the time of day, let alone take an honest interest in her. Hannah was more than happy to spend all of her free time with Lori. It never would have occurred to her to think otherwise.

Hannah had a lust for travel and wanted to go everywhere in the world as fast as she could. She and Lori spent hours on the Internet searching for grant money for travel. There was a ton of grant money out there, Hannah learned early on. Lori did not share her passion for travel, but was happy to go along with anything that Hannah had in mind. She could do no wrong in Lori's mind.

The two set off to Spain together on their first overseas trip. Second semester they ventured to China. Hannah dragged Lori with her everywhere and the two had a wonderful time together exploring the world.

The two were inseparable that first year of college. Hannah even took Lori home with her to Staunton to stay with her family on all of their breaks. Hannah's family welcomed Lori as if she were one of them. This was heaven to Lori who had never felt that she was part of a family before. Hannah's two brothers treated her as another sibling, giving her no breaks or special treatment. Lori never said much about her family, and Hannah decided that it was best to leave the topic alone.

During the summer after freshman year, Hannah took a trip, alone this time, to India. She stayed there through the entire first semester of her sophomore year. She was working for the Peace Corps and loving every minute of it.

While she was away, Lori was assigned a new roommate. The two women stayed in touch, though it was never the same.

Hannah continued to travel throughout the rest of her college career, grabbing whichever grant was available and seeing as much of the world as possible. She not only had a deepened love of travel, but a desire to help those in third world countries. She had set her sites on a career of International Law.

Chapter 3

Snow White's sleep was induced by a bite of poisoned apple.

Three years after graduating from Georgetown, Hannah was back in the United States and decided to give Lori a call. Hannah explained that she was back in the area, attending graduate school and wanted to catch up with Lori. Lori was thrilled to hear from her and to hear all about her exciting adventures. She had been quite disappointed not to hear from Hannah over the last years, but she did her best not to show her disappointment. Hannah made plans to visit Lori the following weekend. The two would have plenty of time to catch up.

Hannah arrived at Lori's tiny apartment with a small duffle bag in hand. She looked just the same, if not better. She glowed with an enthusiasm for life and was more physically fit than she had been in college. Lori, on the other hand, had not fared as well. She looked tired, worn out and just plain fat. Hannah did not care how Lori looked, she was just happy to reconnect with her old friend.

Once inside the apartment, Lori opened a couple of beers and the two sat down for a long catch up session. Hannah started by describing the year and a half that she had spent in India. Lori listened intently as Hannah spent the next two hours describing her many adventures since their freshman year.

Hannah had discovered two loves in India, helping those in need and a young man named Jack. Lori was surprised to hear that she had been in love. Hannah had always made it very clear in college that she found boys her own age to be uninteresting and that she had no plans for love to interfere with her life until she was much older and finished with her travels. The relationship had lasted a year and Jack Wilson ended up returning to his home in New Zealand. They had parted as friends and had no plans to reunite in the future.

Hannah had seen much of the world in the past six years, thirty countries in all. As far as she was concerned, her travels had only just begun. She was only back in the U.S. to complete a graduate degree in International Law so that she could ultimately travel the rest of the world.

Lori dreaded telling Hannah the boring tale of her life over the past six years. She had finished her undergraduate degree and had been working ever since in a law office as an assistant. She hadn't been anywhere or done much of anything. She'd had one brief relationship, with the attorney that she now worked for. They were great friends, and her boss liked spending time with her, but thought of her more as a buddy than a love interest. Lori did have an active social life, mostly with the local gay community. She went out drinking several nights a week with her gay male friends and frequently threw lavish dinner parties for them. Hannah listened, without interruption, thinking that Lori's life sounded fun and interesting.

Lori informed Hannah that she had made arrangements for them to meet her gay friends at a local dance club.

Hannah thought it sounded like great fun. She rarely had an opportunity to dress up even though she loved to.

Hannah spent the next hour in the bathroom getting ready. She looked amazing when she came out, nothing like the fresh scrubbed girl that everyone was used to. Now Hannah was all glamour, smoky eyes, slicked back hair, over-the-knee boots with a mini skirt and lots of layered jewelry. She was stunning! Lori had never seen Hannah like this and was once again ambivalent: she was proud to have such a stunning friend, but envied her at the same time.

Getting Lori dressed for an evening out, was not such an easy task. Her large girth made clothing options limited. She normally chose long tops with several layers, trying to mask her ever-expanding waistline. She did manage to do a nice job on her makeup most of the time, but never changed the style of her plain, brown shoulder length hair. They made an odd looking couple, but didn't care as they were only determined to have a good time.

Lori's friends were waiting for them at the bar when they arrived: five gay men dressed to the nines. Hannah made an audible giggle when she met them. Somehow, they tickled her funny bone. Lori's friends fawned over Hannah, commenting on her appearance. They immediately loved everything about Hannah and asked Lori where she had been hiding her.

Hannah took an immediate liking to one of the men in particular, Josh, and vice versa. Josh had a geeky quality about him that Hannah found endearing. He stood about 5'10", with short, strawberry blond hair, spiked with too much gel, and clear light green eyes. There were traces of light freckling on his pale white skin. His was thin to the point of being boney and he cocked his head to the right side when he smiled.

Hannah was whisked on to the dance floor by one of the men, and then another and another. She occasionally made it back to the table to have a sip of her cocktail, but for the most part spent the entire evening on the dance floor. Lori was having a good time as well, dancing the night away with her friends. Before they knew it the bar was closing and it was time to go home.

Everyone hugged goodnight, and the men insisted on seeing Hannah again before she left on Sunday. Lori offered to throw one of her famous dinner parties the next night. All readily accepted the invitation. Hannah was looking forward to experiencing one of the dinners that she had heard so much about. The two women immediately scrubbed the thick makeup off of their faces upon arriving home. Lori made up the sofa for Hannah. The two revisited the evening's events, giggling all the while. They both fell asleep quickly and slept hard for the next ten hours.

The two spent a leisurely couple of hours in their pajamas the next day as they sipped coffee and reminisced about the old days. Lori began to discuss her ideas with Hannah for the evening dinner. Hannah listened with surprise as Lori rambled on about the details in her mind. As she talked, Lori made her way across her small living room to a closet door. As she opened it, Hannah let out a loud gasp. The small closet was loaded with more stuff than Hannah had ever seen! Lori had decorations, party favors, serving dishes, gifts bags, etc.

"What is all of that?" Hannah exclaimed.

"Oh, just my party stuff." Lori responded matter of factly.

"Are you running a side business?" Hannah asked. "I've never seen so much party stuff in my life!"

Lori responded quietly, "No it's just a hobby. I like throwing parties." Lori began pulling things out of the closet, all the while mumbling to herself about the theme of the party for tonight. Hannah just watched in awe, not uttering a word. Lori made a large pile on the floor, and then pulled out a list and started writing, still mumbling to herself all the while. She compiled a grocery list and explained to Hannah that they would need to make a trip to the store.

Hannah was becoming fascinated by what she was observing. "I'd love to help you shop," she said.

The two got dressed and made their way to the local Piggly Wiggly for supplies. Lori plowed through the list like an expert. Hannah offered to help numerous times, but Lori just ignored her.

The shopping cart was overflowing by the time they arrived at the checkout. Hannah offered to help pay for some of the groceries, but Lori refused. Four hundred dollars later, they were loading the groceries into Lori's Ford Focus. Hannah wondered how Lori could afford such an extravagant menu while she was living in such a tiny apartment and driving a small car, but she decided not to ask since it was really none of her business.

Once back at the apartment, the two unloaded the car, two trips each. Lori immediately transformed, pulling pots and pans out onto the stove and barking orders at Hannah to start chopping vegetables. Her theme for the evening, she had decided, was India. The curries would have to simmer for several hours, which gave Lori time to do some party decorating.

She opened the small closet and pulled out some colorful paper lanterns, throw pillows and tons of sequined silk fabric. Lori threw some bright fabric at Hannah and told her that that's what she would be wearing that night. Hannah nodded agreeably.

Lori's apartment was transformed into an Indian den in a matter of two hours. Hannah was impressed with Lori's capabilities and told her so.

"Now", Lori said to Hannah, "it's time for us to transform ourselves."

Hannah had no idea what Lori was referring to, but was happy to go along. Lori spread the fabrics on her bed and pulled out some boxes from under her bed containing various shoes and undergarments. Lori plowed through the boxes, throwing a pair of silver lame shoes and a short white blouse at Hannah.

"Don't get dressed yet," Hannah instructed her friend, "first let's do our makeup."

Hannah followed Lori into the tiny bathroom and Lori immediately went to work on Hannah's face with tons of black eye liner and a red "tika" on her forehead. Lori explained to Hannah that the tika symbolizes Hinduism. Lori quickly went to work on her own face, using the exact same makeup techniques that she had used on Hannah.

"Now we are ready for the best part," Lori explained, "we get to wear the most comfortable clothes in the world." Lori instructed Hannah to follow her lead. She stripped to her underwear, and then pulled a small white blouse on over her head. She then picked up her piece of bright pink fabric and wrapped it around her waist, anchoring the end with a knot: two times around the waist, then a tuck into the knotted fabric and once over the shoulder. Hannah did her best to follow, but was lost in her yellow garment. Lori took over and draped Hannah's fabric as if she had done it a hundred times before. "Now," Lori spoke, "after you see how comfortable you are tonight, you will never want to wear western clothes again!" The two laughed.

They still had a half hour before Josh and the boys were due to arrive. Lori finished the transformation of her small living room. She stacked some furniture in the bedroom, leaving an open space on the floor big enough for a runner and some pillows in lieu of a table and chairs. The lights were dimmed, the Indian music was turned on and the apartment was infused with the aroma of curry. The transformation was complete, and it was impressive!

The boys arrived on time with Kingfisher Indian beer in tow as instructed by Lori. The merriment began the moment Josh and the boys walked in. They were a bundle of party energy as far as Hannah could tell. They all wanted a turn with Hannah, thinking that she was the most interesting thing that they had come across in a long time. Lori watched out of the corner of her eye, all the while pretending not to notice that Hannah was getting all of the attention that normally belonged to her. The group drank and chatted enthusiastically until dinner was served fashionably late. Lori had gone all out, the food was amazing in it's presentation as well as its flavor.

The boys seemed to take Lori's cooking abilities in stride, treating the meal as an everyday occurrence. The group talked and danced into the wee hours until the boys finally decided that it was time for them to head home.

Hannah began the cleanup process in the kitchen, but Lori insisted that they leave it all until the next morning. Hannah was so exhausted that she wasn't going to argue. The two were fast asleep and slept heavily until noon the next day. Fresh and showered, they tackled the mess in the kitchen together until everything was back in its place, including the fabrics and pillows.

It was getting late, and time for Hannah to head back home. She thanked Lori for a wonderful weekend and told her that she hoped that they could do it again sometime.

Lori found it odd that Hannah had enjoyed herself so much. Certainly, Hannah's life must be more interesting than hers, she thought. Lori assured Hannah that she was welcome to come back any time.

Chapter 4

King George V of England poisoned himself with a lethal dose of cocaine and morphine.

Lori and Hannah's friendship was back in full force in no time at all. Hannah was driving the hour and half from Richmond to Alexandria on most weekends. Hannah had no social life in Richmond, so it was concluded that the two would spend all of their time at Lori's in Alexandria. Josh and the boys spent all of their time with Lori and Hannah on the weekends. Hannah felt as though she had been a part of their lives all along. She felt carefree and happy when she was with her friends. Lori enjoyed having Hannah along with the group, though she did sometimes resent Hannah for stepping in to her life as though she had been there all along.

The group partied heavily on the weekends, mostly frequenting the gay bars and dancing till dawn. Hannah's studies had become increasingly demanding and she found that she was in much need of the playtime on the weekends. She ran several miles a day during the week, but found that she still needed a different outlet on the weekends. Pursuing a law degree at Richmond was no easy task, but she was determined to accomplish her dreams.

Lori continued her job at the small family law firm working for her friend, Robert. She was good at her job and Robert trusted her implicitly. She felt as though she could do her job half asleep, it came naturally to her. She and Robert worked well together as a team. They had known one another for so long that they could anticipate each other needs.

Robert was happily single, focusing on building his law practice and spending time with his friends. He had plenty of dates, but no one that he was particularly interested in, that is until he met Angela.

Robert had been away for the weekend in Greenbrier at a golf tournament with a bunch of his buddies. While he was there he met a young woman in the lounge, bought her a drink and then another. The two were inseparable over the weekend.

He was back in the office Monday morning raving about the woman he had just met. Lori was not impressed. She smelled a rat. It was all moving too fast for her comfort. Robert could not stop talking about how beautiful Angela was, how funny she was, and how smart! Lori thought she was going to scream if she had to hear any more about Angela!

Robert went to visit Angela over the following several weekends in West Virginia. He eventually brought her home to Alexandria and introduced her to Lori. Lori was polite, but very surprised by Robert's taste in this woman. Angela was far from beautiful. She was hard looking and tough. It looked like she'd had way too much plastic surgery and wore entirely too much makeup. Her body was skinny, fit and had been nipped and tucked from every angle. This is what Robert found attractive? Lori would have taken him for liking the more natural type.

Lori was not impressed with the conversation either. Angela did not have much to converse about…working out, clothes and jewelry. Pretty boring stuff, Lori thought. She must be great in bed, why else would Robert be interested? Lori hoped that the infatuation would pass quickly. It did not.

Robert showed up at work one Monday morning grinning from ear to ear. He and Angela had eloped over the weekend. Lori felt nauseous. Was he kidding? Angela isn't the type of woman that you marry! What was going on with her boss? She pretended to be happy for him, but was secretly fuming at his stupidity.

Lori did her best to ignore her boss's new marriage, she carried on with her life as usual, working all week and playing with her friends on the weekends. Robert occasionally asked Lori if something was bothering her, but Lori never let on that anything was wrong. Robert was enamored by his bride. She looked great on his arm, and fed his ego every chance she got.

Lori was appalled when the credit card bills started rolling in. Angela was charging up a storm on her new husband's credit cards: clothing, plastic surgery, and "fitness" trips. Lori dutifully paid Robert's bills as always, keeping her thoughts to herself.

It annoyed Lori that she had never seen Robert so happy in all of the years that she had known him. Maybe she really had not known him at all. How could the Robert that she knew be so taken with a woman of no substance? Angela was all fluff. Where was Robert's head? She knew the answer. Robert talked about his bride ad nauseum. Had he forgotten to talk about anything else? Lori wondered. The months passed, and Lori tuned it all out.

Robert showed up to the office one-day beaming with excitement. Angela had just announced that she was pregnant. Robert wanted children more than anything, lots of children. He was so happy with the news that he could not contain his enthusiasm. Lori was less than thrilled. Now, they would never get Angela out of their lives, she thought.

Robert and Angela celebrated their first anniversary. Lori noticed that the bloom was beginning to wear off the rose. Robert was questioning the enormous credit card charges as well as his wife's whereabouts from time to time. Angela frequented the clubs, while Robert put in long hours at the office. He assumed that she was out with the girls, but occasionally was disturbed when he could not contact her on her cell phone at night. Lori had been on top of this for some time. She scrutinized all of the bills and could not help but notice a disturbing change in Angela's spending and phoning habits. There was one number that stood out, and Lori did her homework to find out who it was. All of the evidence pointed to one conclusion – Angela was cheating on Robert. Now the only question was, how would he find out about it?

Lori did not want to be the messenger to Robert's devastating news. She decided to stay out of it and let Robert find out for himself.

It didn't take long. It was becoming more and more difficult for Robert to track Angela down and they were fighting frequently. One day Robert decided to go through the phone bill, and there it was, one number that was called over and over. Robert felt sick as he read it. He wasted no time in confronting his wife.

There was an enormous eruption as Robert handed the phone bill to Angela. Her face turned bright red as she quickly tried to lie her way out of the situation. Robert persisted with his interrogation; he already knew all of the answers, he just wanted to hear them out of her mouth. Eventually, Angela caved and told Robert everything, more than he wanted to know. She told him every detail of her affair with one of the trainers that she worked with. It had been going on for months. Then she hit him with the biggest blow of all…that she was not and had never been pregnant. She only told Robert that she was pregnant to get him off her back. She added that she would never dream of becoming pregnant and ruining her perfect figure.

Robert was devastated. The room was spinning as he tried to digest the news that he was just delivered. He adored Angela more than anything in the world. How could it have all been a lie? How could she have been with another man? Why? He was good to her, and loved her more than anyone else possibly could. And the baby, that was a lie? Why? What kind of person lies about having a baby? Robert was numb as he left their home.

"Get your things and be out by tonight," he said to Angela. She wanted to know about a divorce settlement.

"Don't worry. You will be taken care of." Robert replied.

Robert was lost. He did not know where to go or what to do. His entire life as he knew it was a lie. He didn't care if he lived or died. He just didn't want to feel anything. He drove to his office and lay down on the black leather sofa, he did not move for two days.

Lori showed up for work Monday morning, and found Robert disheveled on the sofa. He was obviously in a bad state and Lori had a good idea of what had transpired. "What happened, Robert?" Lori asked.

Robert could barely speak, "It's Angela. She cheated on me and she lied about the baby."

"I'm so sorry, Robert." she said, "You deserve better than this."

Robert wept.

Chapter 5

6,563 poison consultation calls are handled on an average day by local poison centers.

Lori managed to talk Robert into leaving the office and letting her drive him home. He did not want to go home, but really had no other place to go. He did not speak on the 20-minute ride home.

Lori was concerned. She had never seen him like this. She suggested that Robert take a shower and get cleaned up. He agreed without resistance. Lori went to work, while Robert showered, scanning the kitchen to see what food was in the house and quickly made a list of necessary supplies.

After Robert had cleaned himself up, Lori got him situated on the sofa in the den in front of the television. He had put on an old t-shirt, plaid flannel pajama bottoms and some beaten up old slippers. She told him that she would be running to the Piggly Wiggly and would be back shortly. He nodded, not listening to what she was saying.

Lori was a woman on a mission. She wasted no time stocking up at the grocery with Robert's favorite foods and magazines.

When she returned, Robert was sitting on the sofa, with a large envelope in his hand. He was catatonic.

Lori asked, "Robert, what's going on? What happened while I was gone?" Robert handed the envelope to Lori without altering his stare or speaking.

Lori took the envelope and let out a loud gasp when she saw what was inside. There were several 8 X 12 color photos of Angela and a man. They were graphic pictures of the two of them having intercourse as well as some nude profiles of the very fit and well-endowed male lover. Robert had never felt this awful in his entire life.

"Where did these come from, Robert?"

"I hired a private investigator to follow the bitch as soon as I got wind of the affair, just in case she did not confess. They were just delivered to the house while you were gone."

"Oh Robert, I'm so sorry. Did you read the report in the envelope?"

"No, not yet. I'm having a difficult time processing what I've seen so far."

Lori sat next to him and held his hand. "I'm so, so sorry."

"It's even worse than you think Lori. Wait until I tell you the whole story, then you are really going to feel sorry for me. I may as well read the report and get the whole thing over with."

Lori handed it to him reluctantly. Robert read the report and made a noise that Lori had never heard before; he was sobbing. He put his head between his legs and sobbed. "I am the biggest damn fool that ever lived! How could anyone possibly be as stupid as I have been?"

He handed the report to Lori. She read it and said, "What a fucking bitch!"

"Give me a minute to compose myself and I'll tell you the whole story, then you will really know what kind of person she is!" Lori waited patiently for Robert to speak. "I can't believe I'm telling you or anyone this. It's so humiliating!"

"You know that anything you say is safe with me. It's okay Robert, I promise."

"Shortly after Angela and I started dating she gave me some bullshit story about having a small vagina, making intercourse nearly impossible. She was a master at giving blowjobs, so I really didn't mind at first. We only had actual intercourse a few times in the beginning. I was shocked and surprised when she said that she was pregnant. It seemed doubtful to me, but not entirely impossible."

"Those pictures prove not only that she was having frequent intercourse, but with a man who is much more well-endowed than I am. Did you see the size of that guy? Small vagina my ass! She can accommodate a horse! The report confirms that those two have been lovers for years. I was just a dupe. She didn't want to have intercourse with me because she didn't want to cheat on him! Could I have possibly been a bigger fool? I mean, really, is that even possible?"

"Don't be so hard on yourself, Robert. You were in love, and we all know what they say about that."

"Yeah, but I was not only blind, but deaf and dumb too! Just shoot me now and put me out of my misery! No more love for me Lori, not ever, never! I am done!"

"Just give it some time; you will change your mind someday. In the meantime, you have a lot of healing to do."

"I don't want to see or talk to anyone for a while, okay, Lori? Will you cover for me for a while, until I start to feel human again?"

"Of course, we will lie low here at your apartment for a while and I will take care of everything. You just rest."

"Thank you." he said, and lay prone on the sofa where he stayed for the next several days.

Lori tried to take care of Robert. She prepared a large pot of Robert's favorite chili and served him a bowl with a bottle of his favorite beer, Red Stripe. He thanked her, but did not touch the chili or the beer.

Lori drove home and quickly packed a small suitcase. She did not want Robert to be left alone in his present state. She informed him that she would be staying in the guestroom for a while and that they would be operating the office out of the apartment until Robert felt like going back to the office. He responded with a grunt. Lori could not tell if he had even heard her.

She had all of the office calls forwarded to the apartment and was able to handle most of the calls on her own, without needing to bother Robert. None of Robert's clients ever needed know what a bad state he was in. They managed to make it through the week.

Lori placed a call to Hannah suggesting that she not come down that weekend. Lori disclosed every detail of Robert's situation.

"That's horrible!" she said. "That poor man." She was disappointed, but agreed to come down the following weekend.

After five days of living on the sofa and not eating, Lori decided that it was time to do something. She managed to talk Robert into going for a walk. It was a beautiful day, and the walk actually made him feel better for a moment.

He did not have much to say as Lori chattered on about various clients who had called throughout the week. Robert was not listening. In his head, he was playing over and over in his mind the image of his wife with another man. He felt lifeless.

The walks continued every day and Robert began to open to Lori about what had transpired in his marriage. She listened patiently and let Robert do most of the talking.

By the end of the second week, Robert was feeling well enough to go back to the office. He thanked Lori profusely for getting him through the worst time of his life. She suggested that he keep his buddies around for a while, perhaps inviting college friends to come visit on the weekends. Robert liked the idea.

By Monday of the following week, Robert was back in the office, going through the motions. On the outside, everything seemed normal, but on the inside, Robert was a changed man. He was now damaged goods. Lori kept an eye on him, making sure that he had plans with his friends as frequently as possible. He went out most nights and always had a buddy or two to party with on the weekends. He did not feel like partying, but it was better than sitting home alone and thinking about Angela. His hurt was turning into anger.

Lori was spending a lot of time with her boss. They went to lunch several times a week and had drinks after work as well. She liked taking care of him; it made her happy that he needed her. Robert thanked Lori often for getting him through his rough patch. She loved the praise. Things were good for her. She was happy at work, happy taking care of Robert and she had her friends on the weekends. This was as good a life as she had ever known.

The next six months passed without event. Lori went to work, kept Robert busy and partied with her friends on the weekends. Hannah was not coming as frequently on the weekends as her classes in Richmond were becoming more and more demanding.

Robert was depressed, but managed to put on a smile for most of the outside world to see. He had drawn up a quickie divorce for Angela to sign. The whole thing was over in about two weeks. Robert had been generous to Angela, so she went away without any argument.

Chapter 6

61 local poison control centers operate in the United States.

Hannah was fully immersed in her studies. Law school was challenging to say the least. She had her nose in a book most of the time, saving her social life for the weekends with her friends in Alexandria. She was spending more time training for marathons and found that the training was a welcome distraction from her studies. She was becoming increasingly focused in her life, on her studies and on her athletics.

Her Alexandria friends often questioned her as to why she never dated. After all, she was very attractive, not to mention funny and intelligent. She always said that she had no interest in dating and that was the end of it.

She was enjoying the intensity of her life and the mindless laughter on the weekends. It was a combination for her that worked, and she wasn't inclined to change a thing.

Lori was opening Robert's mail one morning, as she always did and she mentioned to him that there was a Bar Association dinner in DC coming up and that his presence would be required.

"Damn," he said, "I hate those stuffy dinners. Will you go with me?"

Lori double-checked the date. "I can't that day," she said, "my father is having surgery and I have to be there."

"Father?" Robert questioned. "I didn't even know that you had a father, or any other family for that matter. In all of the years that I've known you, I've never heard you mention one thing about your family."

"That's because they are not worth mentioning." Lori responded. Robert took the hint to drop the subject, though he was more than a little curious now.

"If you can't go, then please find me a suitable date for the evening. No set up, just a date. I never want to get involved again, as you know."

Great, Lori thought, now I'm stuck finding a date for him. Somehow, she didn't recall dating services as part of her job description.

"I'll see what I can do." she responded, having no idea who she could possibly find to go out with him.

Lori and Robert were spending more and more time together. She cooked for him all the time and gave him advice about his life. He said he would never get close to a woman again and she encouraged him to stay away from dating. She liked having him all to herself. She had a built-in companion with him and he always paid for everything. She loved that he depended on her these days. He was generous with her to a fault.

One day after work, Robert drove Lori home. Her car had broken down for the zillionth time. Car maintenance was something that eluded her. As they pulled in front of the apartment, Lori noticed a new silver Toyota 4 Runner with a big red ribbon on it.

Robert exclaimed, "That's for you. Just a small thank you for getting me through the worst time of my life."

Lori was elated as she leaned over to give him a big hug. As she hugged him, she leaned in a little closer and caught him off guard by kissing him on the lips with a fully open mouth.

Robert immediately pushed her away. "Wait a minute," he said, "I think there has been some kind of misunderstanding. We are   just friends and always will be. We tried the dating thing, remember and it didn't work. I just want you to have reliable transportation, that's all."

Lori played it cool. She said, "I'm sorry I was just excited. I didn't mean anything by the kiss. I just wanted to thank you."

"Okay, sure, no problem." Robert put it out of his mind.

Lori jumped out of the car and ran over to check out her new car. "Thank you Robert. This was so thoughtful of you."

"No biggie," he said. "After all, I make a really good living as an attorney and I'm more than happy to help you in any way that I can."

Lori was delighted to hear this. The two celebrated by taking the Toyota to the Tiffany Tavern, one of Lori's favorite hangouts. They were quickly joined by Josh and the boys all hanging out at the bar.

Robert had met "the boys" once or twice, but had never really talked to any of them. This was a part of Lori's world that he knew little about. Josh and the boys made Robert feel welcome, ordering him a beer and offering him a stool at the bar. Robert was happy to be there.

Josh initiated the conversation with Robert. "Sorry to hear about your divorce man. That must have been rough."

"Thanks." Robert responded. "It sure was no fun."

Josh continued, "All that weird stuff she put you through in bed, that must have been real demeaning. I mean not even allowing you to have penetration with your own wife. That must have been harsh." Robert's face turned bright red.

"What are you talking about?" he asked.

"Oh you know, all of those crazy lies that she told you while she was having sex with her donkey boyfriend the whole time. Lori told us all about it."

Robert's blood was boiling, though he did he best not to show it. "Oh that," he said, "yeah, that was really something." Robert quickly changed the subject.

The group stayed at the bar for several hours, drinking beer and ordering greasy appetizers. Lori was laughing and enjoying herself. Robert appeared to be relaxed, but he was so angry that he could hardly see straight. The group said goodnight and Robert and Lori got in the new Toyota.

"Who in the hell do you think you are?" Robert screamed at her. Lori was in shock. She had known Robert for many years and had never heard him raise his voice.

"What are you talking about Robert?" she asked.

"How dare you tell your friends the intimate details of my marriage. I told you things in confidence and I certainly expected them to stay in confidence. I don't know if I can ever trust you again."

"Please, Robert," Lori cried, "it's all just a mistake. It will never happen again. I was drunk one night and they asked me about it. Honestly, I would never betray your trust."

Robert took a deep breath, "I'll have to think about this Lori. We will talk more about it later." The two rode home in silence.

Chapter 7

2.4 million human poison cases were reported in 2003.

The atmosphere was cool between the two the following morning at the office. Robert was still so angry with Lori that he could barely look at her. Lori guessed that she had some quick maneuvering to do to get back into his good graces. She knew just what to do.

"I have that date for you," she said.

Robert was caught off guard. "What date?"

"The one for the Bar Association dinner in DC next month."

"Oh that. Thanks." Robert focused back to the massive piles of papers on his desk. Lori just smiled to herself. She knew that once he saw his date, that she would be out of hot water with him.

The tension dissipated between the two over the following weeks. Things slowly went back to normal, spending most evenings together during the week. Robert had given Lori the benefit of the doubt on spilling his secrets. Surely she had his best interest at heart and would never do anything to hurt him intentionally.

The day arrived for the Bar dinner. Lori informed Robert that she had booked a room for his date at the same hotel where the dinner was to be held, the Ronald Reagan. He didn't ask any questions, just did as he was told. He put on his tux and headed North to DC.

Fifteen minutes later he arrived at the hotel. Lori had arranged for the two to meet in the lounge and she told Robert to look for a blond wearing a red dress. A giant smile spread across his face as he took in the entire package that stood in front of him on the other side of the room.

He walked up to her and she said, "Hi, I'm Hannah," as she presented her hand to shake his.

Robert was still assimilating the blond hair, warm eyes, and expressive smile in front of him. He presented his hand to Hannah and said, "Robert Graham. Nice to meet you." He did not take his eyes off Hannah for a moment. She was perfect. A red satin dress accentuated her athletic curves. She looked elegant in black velvet pumps, bare legs and a simple strand of white pearls around her neck. Her golden blond hair had recently been cropped to a simple graduated bob that accentuated the loose natural curl of her hair. She wore makeup, but not too much.

Robert was pleased. Who was this woman, and why hadn't he ever met her before?

Hannah found Robert to be quite handsome in his tux. At six feet, he towered above her, even with her heels. She was instantly drawn to the warmth of his brown eyes. His face was friendly and open. He was all-American through and through. The two clicked instantly; they both felt it as they headed out the door.

34

There was no lack of conversation as they had a drink before dinner. Robert was full of questions. Where was she from? Where did she go to school? Siblings? Studies?

Hannah responded with more questions of the same. They found that they had much in common, similar backgrounds, likes and interests. There was no doubt about a physical attraction, and the conversation was comfortable and relaxed.

The two held hands as they entered the convention center at the Ronald Reagan Hotel. The evening flew by. The two talked as if they had known each other their entire lives. The conversation flowed with those around them as well. They talked and laughed as if neither had a care in the world.

Before they knew it, the evening was over. It was time to say goodnight to Hannah.

Robert felt a slight sense of panic as he walked her to the hotel lobby. Now what, he thought. He really liked this woman and he hadn't planned on ever feeling anything for anyone again. He had to see her again, but his mind was telling him to let it go. "Don't go there, man." he heard over and over again.

His mind raced as they approached the lobby. "May I see you again?" he asked.

She smiled and said "Of course."

"Good. I'll call you during the week and maybe we can see each other over the weekend."

"Great." She responded as she landed a kiss on his right cheek.

"Thank you for a wonderful evening." she said.

"You're welcome. Talk to you soon." he responded.

Hannah smiled as she entered the elevator. She had a really good feeling about this man. She knew that she would see him again and that it would all be good.

She wondered why Lori had never introduced them before. Lori certainly had disclosed every detail of Robert's life and his divorce to her. She decided that she wanted to get to know all about him first hand, not from Lori's stories.

Chapter 8

52% of all poisonings occur in children under the age of six.

Robert called Hannah a couple of days later. They planned for him to come to Richmond over the weekend. He would come down for the day. Weather permitting, they could kayak on the James River and go out for a nice dinner. Hannah couldn't remember the last time that she had an actual date. She really liked Robert and was willing to break her intentional long dry spell for him.

Lori asked Robert how the date had gone and he didn't say much. "How come you never introduced me to her before?"

"You weren't ready to meet anyone, remember?"

"Oh yeah." he said. Lori was pleased that things had gone well. Now she was out of the hot seat with Robert. After all, why shouldn't her two best friends get together? They could all be together now and have fun doing things as a group. Lori was surprised when Robert told her that he was going to see Hannah over the weekend. She thought that he was done with women.

Robert headed down to Richmond early Saturday morning. The weather was gorgeous; they would have a great day of kayaking. Hannah was ready for him as he arrived on time at 10A.M. Both were dressed in shorts and wet weather gear. Hannah had packed a picnic lunch. Robert thought she looked adorable in all of her REI gear. Hannah had the kayaks strapped to the top of her Volvo station wagon. They were ready to go.

Robert was not as experienced as Hannah, but quickly got the hang of things. They paddled around for a couple of hours before heading to shore for a much needed picnic.

Hannah asked him about his family background. Theirs was very similar, three children in the family, Virginia roots, parents still married and happy. This was unusual. How many times do you meet someone whose parents are still happily married? They enjoyed their baguette, cheese and fruit, with the perfectly chilled bottle of Virginia Chardonnay that Robert opened. It was blossoming into a perfect day.

They relaxed for quite some time before heading back onto the water. They paddled for a couple of hours before calling it a day. They packed the kayaks back on the Volvo and returned to Hannah's townhouse.

The two decided that staying in sounded a lot better than going out. They stopped at Whole Foods on the way home to pick up makings for a barbeque: salmon, salad makings and potatoes. They were done. Hannah had a decent collection of Virginia wines at home to choose from.

Hannah led Robert to the spare bedroom and handed him a towel, pointing to the bathroom. "Do you need anything?" she asked.

"No thanks, I'm all set except for this." He leaned over and gave Hannah a very soft kiss on the lips.

She smiled. "Thank you. See you downstairs in a bit." Hannah was freshly showered and dressed by the time Robert came downstairs and she was building a fire. "You look clean and fresh." she said to him. It was the first time that she had seen him in a pair of jeans and he looked handsome.

Robert was pleased with Hannah's appearance as well. She was in jeans and an off white oversized cashmere sweater. This time, she had a string of gold baroque freshwater pearls around her neck. She was classy and sexy. Robert liked what he saw. Robert had packed a couple of bottles of red wine in his suitcase. He picked one and asked Hannah for an opener. She pulled out a couple of glasses and they toasted to their lovely day together. Hannah directed Robert to the sofa in front of the fire. The conversation picked up just where they had left off earlier. It was comfortable and carefree.

Once again, the time was flying by and it was time to get dinner going. They worked well together in the kitchen. The dinner was delicious. They headed back towards the fireplace after the meal.

The tension between them had been building since they first met and Hannah could no longer contain herself. She wrapped her arms around Robert and pulled him in towards her to give a long, languid kiss. Their passion ignited and the kissing was surprisingly heated. Hannah felt as if she had found her home in his strong arms. The kissing continued for a lengthy time, neither wanting to pull away from the passionate embrace. Hannah was thoroughly enjoying the kiss, but did not want to lead

Robert to think that anything more would be happening that night. It was much too soon for her.

She pulled away first, still holding him in embrace. The intensity of their kissing had taken them both by surprise. They sat on the sofa and talked a bit but it wasn't long before they were on the floor kissing again.

Hannah stopped as things began to progress. "I don't know you well enough yet," she said. "Maybe we should call it a night."

Robert agreed. Hannah insisted that he sleep in the guest room. He did not challenge her suggestion.

"We'll go for some breakfast in the morning before you head back to Alexandria?" she asked.

"That sounds great. Goodnight." He hugged her tightly and gave her a brief kiss on the lips.

Chapter 9

The most common poison exposure for children under the age of six are cosmetics and personal care products.

Hannah was making coffee when Robert came downstairs in the morning. She handed him a cup of coffee and they sat on her small deck as they watched the kayaks go by on the waterway in front of her townhouse. Robert held her hand as they sipped the warm brew. They walked to a local greasy spoon for breakfast, sharing bites of one another's meals.

They walked back to Hannah's, holding hands and not saying much. There was no mention of seeing one another again. Robert placed his small bag into the trunk of his black BMW 750. He put his arms around Hannah and she returned his affections by initiating a long, torturous kiss before he hit the road.

"I'll call you," he said. With that, he was gone. Hannah smiled, knowing that they would be together again soon.

For the next three months, the two saw each other every weekend, alternating going from Alexandria to Richmond. They hiked, went wine tasting, cross-country skiing, etc. They were like a couple of kids who played well together. Hannah stayed at Lori's the first few times that she went to see Robert in Richmond. She stayed there until she was ready to take their relationship to the next level.

One weekend Robert had booked a room for them at the Inn at Old Virginia in Staunton. The two spent the day hiking and wine tasting in the area. They had a lovely meal at Zynodoa in the quaint downtown area. It had been a perfect day. They headed back to their spacious room at the Inn and Robert built a fire. He opened a bottle of Pinot Noir that he had purchased at the Naked Mountain winery that day.

They wasted no time in engaging in a passionate kiss. Robert hastily pulled at Hannah's blouse forcing all of the buttons to come undone at once. His large hand made its way under her white lace bra. With one hand he cupped her breast, and with the other he reached behind her tugging at the hooks. Hannah reached both of her hands behind her to help with the removal of the garment. Robert quickly leaned in placing Hannah's bare breast into his mouth as he held both breasts with his strong hands.

Robert grabbed Hannah by the waist and lifted her onto the nearby desk. She braced herself with both hands as Robert hastily yanked at her pants removing them as quickly as possible. Hannah tugged at Robert's jeans, pulling them down as far as she could reach, to his thighs. He pulled his undershorts with one hand as he grabbed a condom from his pants pocket with the other. He hesitated momentarily to apply a condom and was instantly inside Hannah's warm flesh. Hannah moaned with elation. She had nearly forgotten the incredible sensation of intercourse.

The tension had been building for two months and they could wait no longer. Robert held out as long as he could, making sure that Hannah had reached orgasm before he had one of his own. He pulled Hannah to the bed and held her in his arms as they both fell fast asleep.

It wasn't long before they woke and repeated just as passionately as before. They held each other all night. Their lovemaking was intense and comfortable at the same time. They made love again in the morning. It had been a wonderful weekend. Hannah was as content and happy.

Chapter 10

Although children under the age of six are most commonly exposed to poisons, they represent only two percent of fatalities.

Lori was beginning to feel left out and frustrated. Not only were her two friends not including her in anything, they were not telling her anything about their relationship either. She wanted to know what was going on between them and it was starting to make her nervous that perhaps they were becoming too close and she would be left out in the cold. She wanted Robert to depend on her completely. She could not lose him again to another woman.

She did her best to pump Robert for information at the office about his weekends, but he did not bite. She tried tricking Hannah into giving her information, and she started dropping hints about Robert seeing other women.

Hannah sensed what she was doing and was not amused. There was no way that Lori was going to give up the good thing she had going with Robert. He depended on her and she gained financially by their relationship. He had even hinted about including her in his will.

As Lori's frustration grew, so did her waistline. She had gained 20 pounds during the first few months that Hannah and Robert were dating. She was out every night pounding beers with the boys, becoming angrier and angrier at the lack of control that she had in this situation. How dare they shut her out! This was going to require some serious planning on her part. She would stop their relationship no matter what!

Hannah and Robert continued their back and forth over the following weeks. They had planned a big hiking weekend in Staunton again.

Robert called to say that he couldn't make it. He wasn't feeling well. Hannah was worried; Robert had the constitution of an ox.

He had been throwing up for a couple of days and couldn't shake it. He ended up staying home on the sofa. Lori did not miss her opportunity to play nurse. She brought him soup and kept a cool towel on his head. She stayed and watched movies with him all weekend. He felt as good as new by Monday morning.

Hannah came up the next weekend. They spent Saturday four wheeling with a couple of Robert's friends who owned some property near Front Royal. They decided to stay in the rest of the weekend, just cuddling together. There was no talk of commitment between them. They were just enjoying one another's company. Things were happy and carefree.

They had plans to go to a Dave Matthews concert in DC, but then Robert became violently ill and was unable to get out of bed. Hannah wanted him to go to the emergency room, although he refused. He seemed better by the next day.

Robert's sudden illnesses increased in frequency, but not in duration. Hannah was convinced that something was seriously wrong with him. She feared for his life and begged him to see someone. He eventually agreed.

He went to his general practitioner who found nothing wrong with Robert, although the illnesses continued haphazardly. Robert continued to see doctors, and his health issues were escalating, although not finding any answers.

Things between Hannah and him were progressing wonderfully. The relationship continued to blossom when he was feeling well.

Chapter 11

89 percent of all poison exposures occur in the home.

Robert was visiting Hannah one weekend in Richmond. They were having a quiet breakfast on her deck, watching the kayaks go by. Robert didn't look right; he was sweaty and nervous.

"Look Hannah, I just want to get one thing straight, I will never commit to you. I was burned once, and I will never let myself go there again. If you are expecting this relationship to go anywhere, you are mistaken. I don't want to see you anymore."

Hannah was shocked and devastated. She knew that Robert had been burned by his wife, but where had this come from? She thought that he was past all of that.

"Robert, that's crazy. We have such a wonderful time together. How can you not want more of that?"

"Love is too painful. I don't want to love you or anyone else ever again."

Robert got up from the table and apologized. He went upstairs, grabbed his bag and left. Hannah was dumbfounded. Where did that come from? She wondered. Why did he change so suddenly? What in the world was going on? She had never mentioned marriage to him, so why was he so scared of commitment all of the sudden? She might never know.

Hannah spent the next several months in near seclusion. She went to school and came home. She did not go to Lori's or even talk to her. She felt betrayed by both Robert and Lori and she somehow wondered if Lori had had something to do with Robert's odd behavior. Sad and disappointed, Hannah continued on with her life as she had before, before Lori and her friends, and before Robert. She did not need anyone, she told herself. Somehow this would all make sense one day. She just knew it.

Robert resumed spending time with Lori. She was safe. He did not love her. She could not hurt him.

Lori was elated to have Robert back to herself. She cooked for him at least three nights a week, and they went out for drinks almost every night. Robert talked to Lori about Hannah. He told her everything, all of the details of the relationship. Lori was in heaven. She was back in control. Robert confessed that he was having strong feelings for Hannah, and could not risk getting that close to another woman again. He was determined to have loveless relationships for the rest of his life.

Lori was thrilled to hear this. It would be easy to keep them apart now and she would make sure that they never got back together by setting him up with as many easy women as possible. There was no risk of his falling for a loose woman: the more women between Hannah and Robert, the better.

She wasted no time bending Robert's ear. "It will do you good to get out. I'll fix you up with more of my friends. It will make you feel better. You'll see. Hannah wasn't right for you. You know that she would eventually cheat on you anyway."

"You're right." he said. "Go ahead and fix me up."

That was all Lori needed to hear. For the next few months, she had dates for Robert at least twice a week. She found women who were only interested in one-night stands, the looser the reputation, the better. No chance of Robert getting serious about any of those women. Robert lost himself in the women, for a while.

Robert often brought women back to his place. Each time he bedded a new woman, he felt in control and virile. It was like a drug for him, momentarily erasing the humiliation and powerlessness associated with Angela. The indistinguishable sex made him feel desirable for the time being. Meaningless sex made perfect sense to him. He could never get hurt. The women were there to service him with intercourse, or a blow job, and then he would send them on their way as quickly as possible…no strings attached.

There was only one little problem: Hannah. She was on his mind. The more he tried to forget her and be with other women, the more he thought about her and how he missed every little thing about her. He found himself comparing each woman to Hannah. What had he done? Why had he chased away the one woman who had made him so happy? He expelled those thoughts from his mind and convinced himself that he was doing the only logical thing, the only safe thing.

Lori was thrilled, she felt like a puppeteer. She was in complete control now. As long as Robert was miserable, he belonged to her. Lori was so pleased with herself that she bragged to the boys about it nightly over drinks. She bragged about every detail of Robert's life and how she was responsible for keeping him away from Hannah. She told them that Robert would never make it without her and that he trusted her as no one else that he was going to give her everything that he owned.

The boys just listened. They were becoming used to Lori's bragging and took it all with a grain of salt.

Chapter 12

77 percent of all poison exposures can be treated over the phone by a qualified poison control center.

Several months after the break up, Hannah received a phone call from Josh. "Listen Hannah, I just can't take this anymore. You need to know whom you are dealing with. Please listen to what I have to say."

Hannah replied, "Okay."

Josh talked nonstop for the next two hours. He told Hannah a complete history of Lori, starting with her family background, and it wasn't pretty.

"She comes from a large family, five brothers and sisters. Her father is a very successful, powerful attorney. He physically and verbally abused her from the time she was a toddler until she left home at 17. He isolated her for some reason, inflicting the majority of his rage and anger on her. Her siblings all became very high achieving, successful professionals, leaving Lori to be singled out as the failure of the family. Relentlessly, he berated her, calling her fat and worthless. She's never had a healthy relationship with anyone in her entire life. Thanks to daddy dear, she equates love with money and is ruthless where money is concerned."

"Watch out for her Hannah. She has it in for you." he warned her.

Josh continued on, telling Hannah all about the women that Robert had been sleeping with. Hannah was not surprised, more disappointed than hurt. She thought more of Robert than that. She could not comprehend why he would want to be with women like that after knowing what they had shared together. He's going to end up a lonely, bitter old man she thought.

Josh ended the conversation with another warning about Lori, "Pay attention to the money, it tends to disappear when she is around."

Hannah's head was reeling as she listened to his words. Did she really want to know all of this? It was too late now. She thanked Josh for his honesty and felt emotionally spent as she hung up the phone. What am I supposed to do with all of this information now? She knew that she should completely close the door with Robert. What a disappointment he had turned out to be!

Hannah spent the next few days wading through the hurt and anger she was experiencing. Even though she and Robert had been apart for some time, she still felt betrayed. What they had was real, why would he throw that away for nothing? She had given him her heart openly and trustingly. He had decided to keep his heart closed. And then there was Lori. That situation was becoming so bizarre, and she didn't know what to make of it. Why wasn't Robert seeing any of this yet? He was an intelligent man and he had spent so much time with Lori, certainly he should have had a clue by now as to what kind of person she was.

Hannah decided to leave both Lori and Robert in the past and move on with her life. She set her mind to running a marathon, and when the semester was over, she was going to start her travels again. She wanted to take a year off and go somewhere far away. It would take some thought, but she would find just the right place, the right place to start her life over.

Josh still called her from time to time. She told him that she didn't want to talk about Lori and Robert anymore; it was all too exhausting. Josh apparently needed to unload, so he just kept talking.

The stories about Lori became more and more odd. Josh was telling tales about Lori's strange sex life. Apparently Lori's boyfriend had been confessing to Josh all of the sordid details of their grotesque sexual encounters.

Hannah did not want to hear this, but could not stop Josh from rambling on. "Lori was into some very kinky stuff and was unable to find sexual satisfaction unless she was being verbally humiliated or physically abused. She made demands on her boyfriend in the bedroom that he found disturbingly uncomfortable."

"Lori screamed at him until he complied with her requests for being beaten, choked and told what a miserable, worthless human being she was." Josh said. "The boyfriend finally broke off the relationship, not wanting to continue down such a dysfunctional path. Lori had threatened his life if he dare ever tell anyone the details of their sex life."

This was more than Hannah wanted to know. Hearing Josh's stories made Hannah feel sick to her stomach. Hannah avoided Josh's calls.

Chapter 13

Water is just as effective as a poison antidote as milk.

Hannah received another surprise phone call one day. It was Jack. He was in town from New Zealand and wanted to see her. She was happy to hear from Jack as he had always had a special place in her heart. Jack had been the first great love of her life.

Could she meet him for lunch the next day? Of course she could. She liked Jack and was always happy to see him.

Hannah met him the following day at the Ipanema Cafe, within walking distance from her townhouse. Jack was waiting outside when she arrived. He greeted her with a big smile, his blue eyes twinkling the moment he saw her. He looked happy and relaxed. His sandy blond hair was quite long and he had grown a beard that was a bit on the shaggy side. He looked like he had been at sea for a while, and knowing Jack he probably had been. Jack was a rogue. The look suited him. He was sexy and rugged, yet had a softness about him, like he was a gentle old soul, comfortable in his own skin.

Hannah was surprised to see him dressed up, she was used to seeing him in jeans. This day he wore khakis and a dress shirt. What was going on? She wondered.

The two had a leisurely lunch on the patio. The conversation was superficial, but pleasant. Jack told her that he was in DC trying to get a patent on an engineering idea he had. He would be in town for a couple of days. Hannah explained her plans to leave town soon. She had a million things to wrap up before leaving town for a year. Jack had an appointment, so they concluded their lunch and parted with a friendly kiss on the cheek.

When Hannah got home, there was an email from Jack. It said how happy he was to see her and that she looked beautiful. That didn't sound like him. Jack was never one to use that word. She wondered what was going on with him.

He called later that afternoon and asked Hannah to meet him for an evening on the town. He said that he would introduce her to a couple of places in town where she had never been. Hannah hesitated; she had so much to do.

Finally, she said, "Sure, I'd love to. It sounds like fun Jack."

He responded, "Great, I'll pick you up in an hour." He seemed like a man in a rush. She was happy to be seeing him again.

Jack picked Hannah up at seven. Her beauty blew him away as she answered the door. She wore a black and white floral mini dress, black over the knee boots, and a long strand of white baroque pearls. Her eye makeup was smoky and her lips had just a hint of color. Her hair was loose and wavy. Jack had never seen Hannah like this before. He was speechless.

"Wow Hannah, you look incredible!"

"Thanks."

"Are we ready to go?" With that, they were out the door.

He took Hannah to a wine bar first. There they compared several local Virginia wines to some of Jack's favorite New Zealand wines. It was an eye opening experience for Hannah. They proceeded to the Thai Diner where Jack educated Hannah on some of his favorite Thai dishes. She was impressed with her first Thai food experience.

The two laughed their way through the evening. Jack was a great storyteller, and he had plenty to talk about. Hannah was in awe of his traveling experience. He had seen most of the world, and generally, not as a tourist.

They ended the evening dancing the night away at Club Infusion. Hannah was laughing so hard that she could hardly dance. Jack was a riot on the dance floor, inventing new moves and not afraid to make a fool of himself. They stayed until closing time. He dropped Hannah off at her townhouse before continuing on to his hotel. Hannah thanked him for a wonderful evening.

"Lunch tomorrow before I leave?"

"Naturally! Call me in the morning." She planted a kiss on his cheek and she was gone.

Hannah got ready for bed thinking about what a wonderful evening she'd had with Jack. She always felt safe and comfortable with him. He made her laugh and impressed her with his knowledge of the world. She was definitely happy to see him again and was looking forward to their lunch the following day.

They met for a leisurely lunch at Nacho Mama's. Both were wearing shorts and flip-flops. Hannah looked fresh scrubbed and cute with her hair in a ponytail. They chatted and reminisced for two hours and then they said their goodbyes with a hug with no mention of seeing one another again.

Hannah spent the next couple of days getting her affairs in order. She had made a decision to live in Fiji for a year. She had never been, but knew that she could be helpful building bures for the impoverished local community. She was told that there was a need for breaking horses on the islands and she'd had experience with that as a child. Fiji sounded wonderfully far away from the drama and heartache that was attached to Robert and Lori. She wanted something bigger and better in life than fear and pettiness. She had three weeks to get everything in order to leave for Fiji.

It had been two days since Hannah's lunch with Jack. She received a text message from him; it simply said, "I have an idea."

Hannah's immediate reaction was, uh oh. Jack's ideas were always big and quite imaginative. This would be interesting she thought. She gave him a call.

"Spill." she said.

"I was just thinking of a way that we could see each other again before we both leave the country, and I think I've come up with a good idea. I'm headed down to the North Carolina to visit some old friends who own a riding camp there. We're planning a three-day ride. Why don't you come along? I know how much you love to ride and we could spend some more time together. You'll love my friends. Come on, it'll be a blast."

Hannah immediately responded, "No." She thought the idea sounded crazy. She had way too much to do. No way. Jack kept talking. Hannah kept refusing. Jack wasn't giving up. Jack continued to call her from the road as he was headed to the ranch.

"Come on Hannah, you can take a couple of days and you always love to try something new and you know how much you love to ride." Jack said. He knew how to get to her.

She surprised herself and said "Okay Jack." Next thing she knew she was in her car driving the five hours to Boone.

Chapter 14

74 percent all poisoning deaths were unintentional in 2007; nine percent were undetermined.

Hannah arrived at the ranch in her Volvo station wagon just about dark. There was a large group of people barbequing outside the main house with lots of noise and laughter. Jack's face lit up the moment he saw her. She looked adorable in her riding gear: jeans, a western blouse and cowboy boots. Her hair was in a braid, and her face looked freshly scrubbed. Jack was always surprised at how many different looks she had.

Hannah was offered a gin and tonic the moment she arrived. It looked like everyone had been enjoying the cocktail hour. Jack introduced Hannah around to everyone. It was mainly a large family that owned the ranch plus some longtime friends who would be joining them on the ride. They immediately made Hannah feel comfortable and at ease.

Jack gave Hannah a tour of the ranch. He took her to the barn first. The horses were prepared for the long ride; they would be leaving at dawn. Hannah was impressed with the obvious care that the horses had been given and could tell that the Miller family had put much time and care into the upkeep of the tack.

Jack showed Hannah to her sleeping quarters. She dumped her backpack and they returned to the group, having cocktails, appetizers and laughing at the numerous stories being told. It was a boisterous group, everyone trying to top each other's stories. She liked these people immediately and felt right at home.

Dinner was steak on the grill, corn on the cob and salad. There were several bottles of bold Cabernet wine to go with the steaks. Everyone pitched in with the cleanup, and it was off to bed early. The departure time was set for 5:30A.M.

The bell rang at 5:00. After a quick splash of water on her face, and brushing her teeth, Hannah arrived at the kitchen with the rest of the group. They had time for a strong cup of coffee and a cinnamon roll before heading to the barn. The horses were all saddled and ready to go. Trail riding was the Miller's business and they were well prepared. A wagon would follow the group and would be carrying their supplies and food.

The group of 18 rode through the Blue Ridge Mountains for the next three days. They rode all day except to stop each day for lunch that was prepared for them by the crew. They stopped at 4:30, set up camp and settled in for a night of food, drink and laughter. Hannah loved sleeping on the ground in her sleeping bag next to the fire. She was having a wonderful time.

Jack made sure to stay close to Hannah on the rides. Both were experienced riders, but he was mostly interested in keeping Hannah's attention. He talked to her about anything and everything. On the third and last day of the ride, Jack intentionally kept Hannah at the back of the group with him. "Hannah, have you noticed what a great time we always have together?"

"Well, yes, Jack, as a matter of fact I have noticed." she responded sarcastically.

"Seriously, Hannah. I enjoy your company more than anyone else's, always have." He now had her full attention. She knew that something was up.

"I've thought a lot about us Hannah. I'm at a point in my life where I want to get married and have kids, and I think it should be you and I getting married. What do you think?"

Hannah was stunned. She had thought that the romantic side of their relationship was over long ago. She thought that they were just friends.

"Jack I don't know what to say. You've caught me completely off guard."

"Promise me that you'll give it some serious thought."

"I will Jack. I promise."

Hannah was deep in thought and quiet for the rest of the day. There were many things that she liked about Jack's idea. They had been in love, so there was an attraction. They were great friends and they both loved to travel. This could be a really good thing she surmised. Jack watched her intently, but left her alone. He knew when not to push her.

They returned to the ranch and Hannah thanked everyone for a most wonderful time. She promised to stay in touch. Jack walked her to her car. "Promise me you will let me know soon Hannah. I'll be waiting."

"I will Jack, I will." He hugged her and delivered a toe-curling kiss that she would remember for awhile.

Hannah now had two weeks to close everything up before leaving for Fiji. She had found someone to sublet her townhouse for a year, and she put all of her classes on hold until her return. She would still have a year left when she returned. She rented a storage unit large enough for her car and some of her possessions. She would be traveling light to Fiji. Her papers were all in order, so it looked like everything was a go. She was looking forward to putting the pain of Robert and Lori behind her for good.

Chapter 15

Men are twice as likely to die from poisoning as women.

Hannah spent the next week wrapping up all of her loose ends. Everything was in order by the time she left for Nadi, on the main island of Viti Levu in Fiji. She had a lot on her mind. The situation with Jack was driving her crazy. She wished that she could just say yes to him and get on with having a happy life. She knew that she was having trouble letting go of Robert, but why? He was out of her life. Why wasn't she able to let go completely of Robert? Why did she still love him? She knew that he was a good man who was going through some emotional issues. If he ever worked through them, she knew that they could have an incredible relationship. She had not imagined what was between them, neither did he. That's precisely why he ran away.

Hannah decided that she had to see Jack, and soon, to find out if there was still any chemistry between them. It had been a long time since the two of them were together. She still found him to be incredibly sexy, but had to be sure. After all, this was a decision that would affect the rest of her life. She had a great idea; she would plan a layover in Auckland on her way to Nadi. It was perfect. She proposed the idea to Jack via email and he accepted. Good, she thought. She would know soon enough.

She had an overnight layover in Auckland, Jack flew in to meet her for dinner and spend the night at the Hilton. Hannah was approaching their rendezvous as a scientific experiment. Chemistry or no chemistry; it was that simple. Hannah arrived first, which gave her time to take a shower and change before dinner. They would eat at the hotel. Hannah waited for him at the bar. She looked charming in a blue floral sundress, white sandals and her white strand of pearls. Jack showed up in khaki shorts and a dress shirt. She loved the way he looked, all tan and weathered, with sun streaks in his tousled blond hair.

They ordered a couple of glasses of Australian Chardonnay. The two chattered away as they always did. It was an enjoyable evening. Jack was looking at her intently as if he could read something on her face if he concentrated hard enough. This made Hannah uncomfortable. The meal was fabulous, local lobster as fresh as it comes. After dinner, they took a walk on the beach. It was time for Hannah to conduct her scientific experiment – chemistry or no chemistry. She leaned in for a kiss, but Jack beat her to it. There was definitely still some heat between them.

They walked back to the hotel, Hannah still as confused as before. She was apprehensive about what was coming next. They held hands and quietly walked to their hotel room. Hannah had been with Jack countless times, why was she so nervous? Jack approached Hannah cautiously once in the room. He wasn't at all sure of what she was thinking or feeling at this point and he definitely didn't want to scare her away.

He slowly pulled Hannah in close and kissed her, softly exploring her mouth with his tongue. She moved in closer towards him. The old familiar feelings started coming back to her. There was still chemistry between them. Jack slowly removed Hannah's dress, first running his hands over her shoulders one at a time releasing her straps. He reached around her back with both hands unzipping the garment with a single pull.

Hannah decided to let herself go and enjoy Jack's expertise. He was a formidable lover and knew exactly what to do to please Hannah. He patiently warmed her first with his fingers, tracing her flesh with the lightest touch. He gently teased the tender skin on her inner thighs and around her areola. Hannah closed her eyes, allowing herself to fully enjoy the experience. Jack continued, this time using his tongue over the entirety of Hannah's warm, tanned body, heightening her anticipation.

Jack gracefully placed two fingers inside of Hannah's damp, summery flesh. She arched her back and moaned. Jack patiently played Hannah with his fingers bringing her near orgasm. He then moved his head in between her legs, his expert tongue circling the engorged clitoris and bringing her to repeated climax in an instant. He wasted no time; pulling Hannah's legs up over his shoulders to place his swollen member deep inside. Hannah flinched from the slight pain as he entered. She soon relaxed and was enjoying the experience once again.

Jack flipped Hannah onto her side, pulling himself in close, face-to-face. Ten minutes later, he turned her again, this time face down and bottom up. Once again, Hannah flinched from slight pain as Jack entered her from behind. Jack finished in this position, making sure that Hannah had achieved full orgasm first.

The lovemaking was satisfying, but something was missing, something just didn't feel right to Hannah. She didn't feel the same passion and connection that she had with Robert. Jack played with Hannah's hair as he fell asleep. She missed Robert's expansive arms around her. She lay awake for hours wondering how this would all turn out.

The two had a leisurely breakfast in the morning before heading to their respective destinations. Here she was in Fiji hoping to forget about all of this love stuff and once again it was right in her face!

Chapter 16

The United States holds the record for the highest number of intentional poisonings per year.

Robert had been on quite a binge since breaking up with Hannah. He was drinking heavily every night, going out with Lori mostly. The two were becoming quite a pair, both angry and bloated. Robert was also on a binge with the women. He figured that the more women he bedded, the easier it would be to forget about Hannah. He was mistaken. He found himself comparing every woman to Hannah and, naturally, they all came up short but he could not take a chance with Hannah. There was too much risk there of getting hurt again.

Robert buried himself in work during the day, in alcohol and women at night. He told himself that he was living the dream and that he was happy, and it worked …for a while.

One night he was sitting in a restaurant across the table from what felt like the zillionth woman he had taken out and something snapped. He could not make out the words as the woman across the table from him droned on about her life. Try as he could, he was unable to concentrate on what she was saying. Why would he even care what she was saying? He wondered. Let this date please be over soon, was all he could think to himself.

He took the woman home before she had a chance to know what had happened. When he got home, he called Lori. "Don't set me up on any more dates," he instructed her.

Lori complied, but wondered if she were losing control of Robert.

Robert decided that he did not like himself under the current circumstances, and he vowed to do something about it. The next morning he got up and started running. He ran every day, and cut way back on his drinking. He realized that he had been numb for the last six months and he was tired of it! He understood how he had really screwed things up with Hannah. He had a woman who truly loved him and accepted him for exactly who he was and he gave her up for a string of women who he forgot about 10 minutes later. What a fool he had been!

He signed himself up for a marathon. This gave him some much-needed focus. He was starting to feel alive again. How could he have let Angela rob him of his life like that? She wasn't even close to being worth it!

Lori could see Robert's enthusiasm and drive. This worried her. She liked it when Robert was miserable. She could control and manipulate him easily when he was down. She knew that she would have to find a way to keep him depressed.

As Robert started to feel again, he resumed that old familiar ache for Hannah. What if he had blown it with her? What if it was too late? Every time he thought about it, he put it out of his mind. It was too scary to imagine that he may have chased her away for good. He certainly would not blame her. He had been unfairly cruel and unkind to someone who had done nothing but open her heart to him and enjoy his company.

Robert decided not to try to contact Hannah. If she had moved on, it would be much too painful to deal with. He would just focus on his work and running. He also decided to distance himself from Lori. He was beginning to see her toxicity.

Robert was a little cool toward Lori and did not take her up so often on her offer to do things together.

Lori was very displeased with Robert's new behavior. She vowed to herself that she would have him back in a place where she wanted him, where she was in complete control of him.

Chapter 17

Denmark runs second in intentional poisonings per year.

Hannah took a seaplane over to a small, unnamed island near Moturiki Island. She laughed when she saw her pilot, in shorts with no shoes. She loved it! The entire local population greeted her when she landed, all 50 of them.

"Bula!" they shouted to her. She was struck by the friendliness of the natives as they escorted her to her bure.

The accommodations were clean and simple. She would share a bure, a small house made of straw and wood, with several other young women while working on the island. There were plenty of projects to keep them busy. She would be helping build a school and breaking some horses to start with. Her first job every morning was to break in the horses with one of the local young men, Samu, by riding them around the island. This was work? She was in heaven. It was the first time she had ever ridden a horse barefoot and she couldn't imagine ever going back to riding boots again! She had a very good feeling about her choice to be there. It felt like she was in the right place and it would be a conducive environment to focus on others, not her own petty problems.

She was given a couple of t-shirts and sulus to wear. That would be her uniform. The Fijians, she found, were conservative in their dress; they did not like to show much skin.

The first project at hand was to build a school, a one-room schoolhouse. The children of the island were thrilled that Hannah and the others were there to build them a schoolhouse. Everywhere that Hannah went, there were at least three or four Fijian children at her side. She was enjoying every moment of her experience there.

Hannah was able to communicate with Jack on a daily basis by text message. He was the only one she communicated with besides the occasional text to family members. She looked forward to hearing from Jack, but made it clear to him that she still had not made up her mind about his marriage proposal. She told him not to wait around for her since she was unsure of her feelings. He disappeared occasionally, saying that he did not want to wait for something more any longer, and then he would come back around and ask her forgiveness.

Jack was tenacious in his pursuit of Hannah. He consistently presented her with dangling carrots: a trip to one of the neighboring resort islands, sailing together on a yacht, meeting in Sydney, etc. Hannah was always tempted, but knew that meeting Jack would present an uncomfortable situation. She would be pressed to make a decision.

The days flowed with satisfying work, laughter with children and text messages from Jack. The months were flying by a little too quickly for Hannah's comfort level. She liked where she was and was ambivalent about returning to Richmond and resuming her studies.

Jack was growing weary of his attempts to convince Hannah to be with him. He asked her to meet him in Nadi so that they could have a serious talk face to face. Hannah knew what was coming; it was do or die time. She knew that it was only fair to give Jack a chance.

Jack had booked two rooms at the Novatel Hotel, just in case things did not go the way he hoped. They met in the bar. The place was empty; it was a good place to talk. He ordered a couple of Australian Chardonnays. "Alright Hannah," he said, "I'm sure that you have a good idea why we are here."

"Yes," Hannah replied, "I do."

"I've given this everything, Hannah, for six months now. I love you, and I don't want to put pressure on you, but I've got to know, do I have a chance with you?"

Hannah had convinced herself over the months that being with Jack was the logical thing to do. He would not hurt her as Robert had done. She was safe with Jack. It seemed right. "I have a proposition for you Jack."

He was all ears.

"Let's agree to be engaged when I finish my time here in Fiji, and then we can make it official. At that point we can work out the details of where we will live, etc."

Jack replied, "Done." Jack jumped out of his seat and grabbed Hannah, squeezing her as tight as he could. At least she had made his day, she thought.

It turned out that Jack only needed one room that night. They re-consummated their relationship at the Novatel. The lovemaking was almost identical to the last time that they'd been together. It all felt rehearsed to Hannah. Technically the sex with Jack was good, almost too good, too polished. Hannah still had the impression that he had done the same exact things with countless other women. She felt as if she were just another body in his bed. She knew that he loved her, but where was the tenderness between them? Where was the bond?

They lay next to one another, with Jack stroking Hannah's hair softly. Hannah lay silently in panic. The sex was good, she thought, but she felt no love as she did for Robert. She wanted to cry. She wanted Robert out of her head and out of her heart.

Chapter 18

Homicide poisoning is often intended to mimic some
medical situation.

Hannah and Jack had one more day together before
heading back to their respective responsibilities. They
decided to make the most of it. They hired a guide to take
them horseback riding around the island. The view was
magnificent and the environment serene. It was just the
three of them and a picnic was included several hours into
the ride. Hannah loved to ride horseback and was grateful
that she was able to ride every day while in Fiji. Jack was
an experienced horseman, but not quite the fan of it that
Hannah was.

After the ride, they took some towels and headed to a
private beach. They spent a lazy afternoon watching the
waves and napping. Hannah was relaxed, but still
somewhat on edge about her mixed feelings for Jack. It
would all work out, she kept telling herself. He was a
wonderful man and she would learn to love him again
over time. She was convinced that the feelings she once
had for him would return. If only she could get Robert out
of her mind. Every time Robert popped into her head, she
intentionally changed her thoughts, hoping that eventually
she would stop thinking about him.

Jack and Hannah had a romantic lobster dinner at the hotel with more wonderful Australian Chardonnay. After dinner, Jack presented Hannah with a shell ring that he had purchased from a local vendor at the beach. It was a promise ring he told he: a promise to be engaged in six months.

"I'm holding you to it Hannah."

"I promise Jack, really I do."

They made love that night, but Hannah's heart was not in it no matter how she tried. When she was with Jack she felt uncomfortable, like she was somehow making love to her brother. She liked it better when she and Jack were just friends and communicating from a distance. She felt pressure whenever she was with him.

The same pilot returned to get Hannah and take her home to her little island. She said goodbye to Jack, not knowing when she would see him again and relieved to have some distance between them. Jack looked very happy with himself as they said their goodbyes. He finally was getting what he wanted after all his efforts in pursuing Hannah.

She was happy to be home again on her little island, with the friendly natives and her fellow volunteers. She was looking forward to her morning ride with Samu.

The islanders had a weekly ritual that involved a small-motorized boat to one of the neighboring islands to pay respect to the local medicine man by joining him in a kava ceremony. This became the highlight of Hannah's week. The medicine man was old and sweet, and he and Hannah had developed a kinship over time.

One day the medicine man passed a message on to Hannah through one of the native women. She said, "He says that you have problems with your heart. It makes you sad. You must learn to detach yourself from the one you love, and learn to love yourself. You do not need someone else's love to make you happy. When you do this, all suffering will cease."

Hannah was shocked at his observation. Was it so obvious that she had had her heart broken? She nodded to the medicine man in gratitude and he smiled with satisfaction.

The medicine man's words haunted Hannah. She couldn't get his advice out of her mind. She focused on letting go of Robert…complete detachment.

The next few weeks were a wonderful experience on the island. Hannah bonded with the natives, worked with the horses, visited with the medicine man, and forgot about Robert. No more pangs of hurt, no more ache in her heart. He was gone.

The communications with Jack were limited. He was traveling and frequently unable to communicate at all. Hannah was relieved. She needed a break from thinking about the situation with him. She focused on the horses, the schoolhouse and the children. She was relishing every moment.

About two months after Jack left, Hannah received a text message from her mother in Staunton. Her father had suffered a heart attack and Hannah needed to get home right away. She was numb, her father was only 48 and in good health, as far as she knew. He was still alive, but the situation was grave.

She immediately spoke to the natives asking for their help. They would need to find Mike, the pilot, for her right away. He could take her to Nadi where she could get a flight to Auckland or Sydney and fly home from there. She had no time to waste. She texted her mother and informed her that it would probably take her two days to get home, but she would be there.

Mike picked Hannah up first thing the next morning. She said goodbye to everyone and promised that she would be back soon to finish out her time on the island. She was sad to leave and everyone was sad to see her go. She texted Jack once she arrived in Nadi to tell him about her father. He wanted to meet her, but she insisted that there was no time. He offered to go with her, but she refused. It was a full 30 hours of travel time before Hannah arrived at Dulles in Reston. She then had a two and a half hour drive to Staunton. She was exhausted.

She went directly to the hospital. The entire family was there and her father Charles was not doing well. He made it through the night, but passed the following morning with the entire family at his bedside. Hannah was so exhausted, that she wasn't even sure if his death had really hit her yet. She went home to her parents' house and slept for the better part of the next three days.

Chapter 19

Long term arsenic poisoning causes a vitamin A deficiency
leading to heart disease and night blindness

Robert received an unusual looking letter at his home.
He opened it immediately. It was from a newspaper, an
obituary from The News Leader newspaper from
Staunton. Robert was surprised as he read Hannah's
father's obituary. He had died a few days ago and the
services were to be held the following Friday. There was a
hand written note with the news clipping. It read:

Robert,

I thought you might like to be there for Hannah.

Josh

Robert's stomach ached as the thought of seeing Hannah
came to mind. What if she did not want to see him? What
if she were there with someone else? What if she can't
forgive me? The thought of seeing her again scared the
crap out of him.

He decided that he had to do the right thing and show
up at the funeral. He wanted to be there for her, even if
she didn't want him. He made plans to take the day off
and drive down to Staunton. He made sure not to tell Lori

of his plans. He did not want her to have a chance to screw things up for him. He arrived at the Trinity Church fifteen minutes before the service started and found a seat in the back of the church. He didn't see Hannah anywhere. The family entered from the back of the church and was seated in the front pews. His heart raced when he saw Hannah. She looked tanned and rested, not what he had expected to see at her father's funeral. She looked even more beautiful than he had remembered. He was terrified to talk to her. Not knowing was better than being rejected in his mind.

Robert waited near the entrance of the church when the service was over. He wanted their reunion to be private. It as nearly an hour before Hannah finally pulled away from the mourning crowd. She almost walked right by Robert, when he said, "I'm so sorry for your loss."

Hannah stood motionless, not believing what she was seeing. "Robert?" she asked, "What are you doing here?"

"I came to give you support." He replied.

"But…" was all that Hannah could utter. She took two steps toward him, threw her arms around him and wept. Robert, feeling befuddled, put his arms around her and held her while she cried. They said nothing.

Hannah broke the silence, "I still don't understand what you are doing here Robert. How did you know about my father?"

"An anonymous note." he said.

"I need to go to the house. People are waiting, lots of people. Please come to the house with me, Robert."

"Hannah, I really don't think that's a good idea."

"Of course it is. You came here to support me, and I want your support at the house."

Robert laughed. Even at her father's funeral, she hadn't lost her sense of humor. Robert followed her to the house. He had no idea what to expect when he got there, but at least she seemed happy to see him.

The house was full when they arrive. Hannah politely led Robert around the room introducing him to everyone including her family. He wondered what the family had heard about him and what they must think of him. They were most congenial to him, making him feel right at home. Robert was a social person and enjoyed talking to all of the mourners. The food and wine were plentiful and once he relaxed he actually felt right at home.

Hannah passed by him at one point and said, "You are not going anywhere tonight until we talk." As she kept walking, he felt a slight chill.

The guests started to leave after several hours. Hannah's mother, Amy, offered the guesthouse to Robert for the night but he declined. Her mother insisted. He reluctantly accepted, not knowing what he was getting himself in to. Robert was taken by the strong family resemblance between Amy and Hannah. They looked almost identical except for the age difference. Amy still had a youthful and athletic appearance at 48.

Hannah suggested that they change into more comfortable clothes and relax. She showed Robert to the guesthouse and told him that she would meet him in the screened in porch in 15 minutes. He nodded in agreement.

Hannah was building a fire in the large fireplace when he entered. It was pouring rain outside. She looked so vulnerable, he thought: adorable, in an oversized tan sweater, jeans and Uggs. The sweater was her brother's and was large enough to slide of off her shoulder, exposing her bare skin. Robert felt startled by his response to her bare shoulder. He hoped to conceal his erection from Hannah. She wore a simple pair of large white baroque pearls on her ears, illuminating the sheen of her flesh even more. Robert realized that he was in deep trouble here. He knew at that moment that he loved her.

"Have a seat." Hannah said pointing to the loveseat in front of the fireplace. "I'll be right back." She returned with two glasses and a bottle of local Virginia Syrah. She handed the bottle and opener to Robert and turned to stoke the fire. He handed her a glass of wine and the two sat on the small sofa.

"Thank you for coming, Robert. I don't really understand why you are here, but thank you."

"You are welcome." he responded.

"Spill." she insisted.

"Spill?"

"Yes." she said. "I want to know what's going on. The last time I saw you was close to a year ago, and you were walking out my door. What's going on?"

"I'm sorry, Hannah, about all of that. I was scared. I was having feelings for you, so I ran away. I know I hurt you and for that I'm sorry. Can you ever forgive me?"

"Yes I can forgive you, but I need to know what changed your mind."

"It's a long story, and it's not very pretty. I had a long downward spiral and it took me some time to discover what is important in life and what's not. You are important to me. The rest doesn't matter."

Robert leaned in for a long romantic kiss; Hannah reciprocated. Robert asked, "What about your family?"

"They've all gone to bed. They're exhausted. I'm the only one around here who has had any sleep."

Robert resumed his embrace with Hannah. She had forgotten how safe she felt in his arms. There was much to talk about, but now was not the time. It felt right to be with him and that was all she needed to know for the moment.

It was a wonderful Virginia evening downpour, heavy thunder and lightning. Hannah led Robert by the hand to the guesthouse. They ran as fast as they could, getting soaked with rain and giggling the entire way. Hannah ripped Robert's soaked sweater swiftly off over his head. Robert watched Hannah intently and then he did the same, pulling her wet sweater up over her head. Robert grabbed her, moving his generous hands quickly over her bare, damp skin. He swiftly walked her to the bed, sat her on the edge and pulled the wet jeans off of her body. Hannah waited patiently as he anxiously pulled his jeans away from his damp skin. He leaned over her, kissing her all the while.

He grasped her by the legs and pulled her body to the edge of the bed. He wasted no time speedily placing himself inside of her. She groaned as she felt the familiar warmth of his flesh inside of her. They watched each other's expressions intently as they made love. Their cold, clammy skin quickly turned warm with perspiration. Robert held out as long as he could and did not move when he had finished. He held Hannah tightly as they fell asleep together. She felt safe and at home once again in his arms as the thunder clapped loudly in the distance.

Chapter 20

Succinylcholine paralyzes the respiratory muscles.

Hannah awakened early. She whispered to Robert, "I'm going to sneak in the house. Sleep in, shower and meet me inside for coffee about nine." He grabbed her, pulling her in and giving her a long deep kiss. She was gone. Robert rolled over and went back to sleep with a big grin on his face.

He entered the kitchen at precisely nine o'clock. Hannah was pouring coffee and handed him a cup. The kitchen counter was full of all the food that the neighbors and friends had been bringing all week. Robert chatted with the family. Hannah's mother suggested that they go for a hike and take a picnic later. It sounded great. Everyone hung out in the kitchen for a while, mostly remembering stories about Charles. Robert was sorry that he had never met him.

Robert borrowed some clothes from Hannah's brother and the two of them headed off for their hike. Hannah knew a spot that had a large rock at the top where they could picnic. It felt to Hannah as though they had never been apart. Her time with Robert was always comfortable and easy. He made her laugh like no one else with his quick wit and expressive face. Robert took great delight in making her laugh.

They made the two-hour hike to the top, and Hannah unpacked a blanket from her backpack. Robert opened a nice bottle of crisp Chardonnay. She had packed fruit, cheese and salami. They were hungry after their climb. Robert and Hannah lay on the blanket. She couldn't imagine a more relaxing day. Robert took Hannah's hand as they talked. He started to play with the ring on her left hand. After a moment, he asked, "Where did you get this?"

Hannah's face flushed. She replied, "I'm sort of engaged."

"You are what???" Robert demanded to know.

"I'm sort of engaged."

"What does that mean?"

"It's a long story," she said.

"Well, let's hear it!" his voice was increasing in intensity.

"Robert, please calm down." This was his worst nightmare; exactly what he was afraid of. "Robert, you have no right to be angry with me. You walked out of my life, never once asking anything about my life or me. I certainly heard about all of the women that you've been with."

"What? You heard that from whom? That is none of your business!" Robert was furious. "I want answers, and I want them now!" he demanded.

"We won't get anywhere while you are this angry." she said.

"Fine, let's go."

The hike back down the hill was horrible. Robert had thrown everything hastily in to the backpack and strutted down the hill. His legs and his stride were much longer than Hannah's. She found it nearly impossible to keep up. She begged him to slow down, but she didn't think that he even heard her. She had never seen him like this before and thought it best to leave him alone. They made it down the mountain in an hour, silent all the way. The ride home was even more awkward, not even a peep.

Robert pulled up in front of Hannah's house and opened the door for her. "Tell your brother that I will get his clothes back to him."

"Okay." she said.

He couldn't get out of there fast enough. Hannah was dumbfounded, she didn't know whether to laugh or cry. Why had he come back in her life? She didn't have a clue.

Chapter 21

Poisoning became a popular form of homicide in Medieval Europe.

Hannah made excuses to her family for Robert's quick departure, not letting on that anything out of the ordinary had happened. They all commented that they enjoyed meeting him and thought it was kind of him to be there for Hannah at the service. They hoped that they would see him again. She was wondering if she would ever see him again as well.

She had a couple of days at home with her family before heading back to Fiji. She didn't even want to think about Jack and what a mess she had made of things. She definitely had not thought about what she was doing; she was just following her heart and look what a mess she had made!

She did not like Robert's behavior, but really couldn't blame him for his reaction. He must have been hurt and not able to control his emotions. She hoped that he would be in touch once things settled down, so that they could finally talk things out.

It was bittersweet leaving her family. Things would never be the same with her father gone. She did not want to leave her family, but was missing her new extended family in Fiji. She was determined to finish her time there and hoped that the rest of her life would work itself out over the next few months.

It was another two days of travel back to Nadi and Mike was there to pick her up in his seaplane. She was happy to see him, bare feet and all!

She had not informed Jack of her return, she couldn't chance that he might surprise her and meet her in Nadi. She needed time to figure things out before she could face Jack.

The entire village was there to meet her plane. They were a sight for sore eyes. They all wanted to know about Hannah's trip and how she was feeling about her father's passing. She was happy to be back. She had missed the morning rides with Samu most of all. Everything was back to normal, almost. She limited her communications with Jack. She was now more confused about Robert than ever, but vowed to un-attach herself once again. She focused on being in Fiji and what she was doing there, not the men in her life.

Robert had managed to calm down, though it took awhile. He had to have some answers from Hannah. He had to see her. It took him two weeks to calm down and get up the nerve to go to see her. He left work early on a Friday afternoon, not telling Lori where he was going. He arrived at Hannah's townhouse in Richmond just before dark. He knocked on the door. A petit brunette answered the door. "Is Hannah home?" he asked.

"Who?" He asked.

"Hannah Ellsworth."

"Oh, the woman that owns this place? I'm subletting from her. She's gone for a year. Been gone since last July."

"What?" Robert asked confused. "She's gone? But that doesn't make any sense."

"Sorry," she said. "I can't help you." She shut the door.

Robert didn't know whether to be angry or worried. Hannah was just full of surprises these days. What the hell was going on? Now what?

He had an idea. He had Hannah's brother's hiking clothes in the car. He could take a drive down to Staunton and see if he could get some information from her family. He certainly did not want to ask Lori and tip her off to the fact that he and Hannah had recently reconnected.

Robert had time to think on the two and a half hour drive to Staunton. Where in the world could Hannah have been all of these months? Why didn't she mention anything to him when they were together? Maybe it had something to do with the fiancé. What in the hell was she doing sleeping with me while she was engaged to someone else? Robert had a lot of questions and he wanted answers, now. He wasn't able to focus on anything until he found out what was going on with Hannah.

Hannah's mother, Amy, answered the door. "Robert, how nice to see you. What are you doing here?"

"I came to return Peter's clothes." he responded.

"That was awfully nice of you, but you really didn't have to come all this way just for the clothes. Please come in Robert. Would you like a cup of coffee?"

"I would love that." he replied. This was perfect, Robert thought, he could get plenty of information from a conversation with Hannah's mom.

"I apologize for leaving in such a hurry the other weekend, but something came up."

"Oh, Hannah explained that. Not to worry."

"Where is she by the way?"

"Well she's back in Fiji of course."

Robert was stunned, but tried not to show it. "Do you have her contact information? I seem to have misplaced it."

Hannah's mom wrote down Hannah's phone number and handed it to Robert. "She can only communicate by text. She's on some tiny island and the reception is poor, no phones or emails."

"Does Hannah's trip to Fiji have anything to do with her fiancé?" he wanted to know.

"Fiancé? There's no fiancé. Where on earth did you get that idea? She is there as a volunteer, helping the local community."

Robert was relieved and confused. Why had she told him that there was an engagement? Miss Hannah certainly was full of all kinds of surprises!

Chapter 22

Arabs made arsenic odorless and transparent.

Robert had some serious digging to do. He had to get to the bottom of this situation with Hannah. At least there was no fiancé. That was a huge relief! He went back to the office to do some researching on his computer. He just didn't want to tip Lori off as to what he was doing. Fortunately, Lori had a boyfriend these days. The boyfriend was a bit of a mess, an unemployed druggie, but at least he was keeping Lori out his personal life.

First, Robert checked out the different agencies that he thought Hannah might be working with. Dead end. He contacted University of Richmond to see if perhaps she had set something up through them. Nothing. He spent half the day looking into one dead end after another. There was only one solution – he had to go to Fiji.

He booked himself for the following week. It would take him that long to tie things up at the office. He would have to make up some story to keep Lori off his track. He didn't know if Lori was aware of Hannah's whereabouts or not. She knew his entire family and all of his friends, so he would have to make it business related somehow. It wasn't going to be easy to get to Hannah's remote island, but he knew that he would be able to get to Nadi without a problem.

Everything was in order and he was off to the Dulles airport. He had one small bag and his passport. He would be in Nadi in 26 hours, after three plane changes. He arrived in Nadi and checked into the Sofitel Hotel. He wanted to sleep for the next two days. Before he went to his room though, he inquired about getting to Hannah's little island. The pilot would meet him in the lobby the following day at noon. Robert went to his room and slept until ten o'clock the next day.

Robert was surprised to see his pilot wearing shorts and no shoes. Mike introduced himself and led Robert down the plank to his seaplane. "What brings you to Moturiki Island, mate?"

"I'm going to visit someone." he responded.

Mike asked, "Who could you possibly know on that tiny island. It's nothing but natives."

"No, there's a girl there that I know from home in Virginia."

"Oh Hannah!" Mike exclaimed.

Robert couldn't believe that he was in the middle of nowhere and that the pilot knew Hannah!

"Great girl, that Hannah!" Mike remarked.

Robert suspected that perhaps Mike might have an involvement with Hannah. He was a good-looking guy and there probably weren't too many other men around. He decided to stop the conversation with Mike.

Thirty minutes later, they landed near a small pier on a tiny island. There were 50 or so people waiting at the pier as Robert disembarked. No one knew who was on the plane. Hannah was there and let out an audible gasp when she saw who it was. "Robert!" she shrieked. "What in the world are you doing here?"

"I'm here to see you, of course," he said as he walked towards her with open arms. She ran into his arms, and felt that old familiar safeness there. He gave her a big kiss on the forehead and smiled from ear to ear. "So nice to see you, Hannah."

"Nice to see you, too," she said shaking her head and smiling back at him.

Hannah introduced him around to the villagers. They greeted him with smiles and a friendly "Bula!" Hannah gave him a quick tour of the island and then they walked back down to the pier.

"Okay Robert. What are you doing here?"

"I had to talk to you, Hannah. I need to know what in the world is going on. Why you are here: if you are engaged? I also need to apologize, for my behavior last year as well as my behavior two months ago."

"You've caught me off guard here. I wasn't exactly expecting you and I'm supposed to be working here, not entertaining my boyfriend."

"I'm sorry Hannah."

"Not a problem, we'll just have to put you to work while you are here."

Robert looked a little surprised, but agreed. Hannah went to talk to her supervisor who was thrilled to have some more help. He put Robert to work right away digging the foundation for the school. This wasn't exactly what Robert had in mind when he was thinking of visiting Fiji. Robert worked all day and was able to see Hannah at meals. He wondered if they would ever have time alone together to talk.

After dinner, they walked down to the pier. She explained that the Fijians were very conservative and would not find it proper for the two of them to be alone together. They had to remain in plain sight of everyone. The pier was a good spot.

Robert started the conversation by apologizing once again for hurting her and running out on her last year. She listened quietly as he explained everything that he had been through and why he had behaved the way he had. She said that she had been very hurt by his actions, but got over it and had fully forgiven him.

"I came to your father's funeral hoping to receive forgiveness and to try and work things out. Then you tell me that you are engaged. I overreacted, but I was in shock, Hannah and I still don't understand. And why are you here in Fiji?"

"I came to Fiji to get away from all of the pain associated with you and Lori. I needed a break, a fresh start. I couldn't get you out of my mind and my heart, so I just had to go far away and focus on something good. I'm committed to a year here and I'm enjoying every minute of it."

"Did it work?" he asked.

"What?" she wanted to know.

"Did you get me out of your mind and heart?"

"Yes I did, as a matter of fact, and as soon as I did you appeared at my parents' house in Staunton!"

Chapter 23

Nutmeg can cause hallucinations and can be toxic in large amounts.

Robert ended up spending a week on the island with Hannah. They worked all day, and talked all night. It gave them a chance to really get to know one another and clear the air. They talked about everything, including Jack. Hannah did her best to explain the situation to Robert who was very bent out of shape and jealous. He knew that he had no room to say anything since he was the one who bailed on Hannah and bedded every woman he could find. This was different than his, it was worse. Hannah had a deep emotional attachment to Jack. Robert was scared and worried that he could lose Hannah for good.

The two became closer over the week, bonding while working on the school house and sharing their deepest feelings. This was a comfortable space for both of them. Hannah knew that she was still in love with Robert and this time Robert did not fight his feelings for her.

"Hannah, I love you." he said one night at the pier. Hannah was taken aback.

"I love you too Robert."

He was relieved to hear that from her. He was tired of protecting himself and he knew that he had to share his feelings for her before he lost her again, perhaps forever, if he weren't careful.

"What are we going to do?" he asked her.

"About what?"

"About us?" he asked.

"I want to finish my time here, and then I'll come back to the U.S. and we'll figure it out from there."

"What about Jack?" he asked.

"I will handle that. Don't worry." But, Robert was worried. Two months was plenty of time for Hannah to change her mind.

Hannah had told Robert all about the kava ceremonies with the medicine man and was thrilled to share the experience with him. She explained how the kava ceremonies worked.

"It's a nightly ritual with most Fijian families. Everyone sits cross-legged around a large wooden bowl filled with kava root and water. One person mixes the beverage slowly and then passes a coconut shell filled with the concoction. Everyone takes a sip. The ceremonies can go on for hours, it's very social. There are special ceremonies for weddings and special occasions. The kava makes your mouth slightly numb. The women say that the men believe that they become great lovers when they drink it!"

Robert enjoyed the ritual. As the ceremony was wrapping up, the medicine man said something to the woman next to him. She nodded. The woman walked over to Hannah and whispered in her ear, "He says to tell you congratulations."

Hannah looked at the medicine man and he gave her a wink. She turned beet red and looked at the ground. Robert was watching.

"What was that all about?" he wanted to know.

"I'll tell you later." Hannah replied.

Robert, Hannah and the villagers all headed back to their island in their motorized little boats. Robert was pleased with the experience. He could see why Hannah was enjoying herself on the island, though it was not an involvement that he would choose for himself.

Hannah arranged to take a couple of days with Robert in Nadi before he headed back to Richmond. They needed some time alone. Mike picked them up and flew them over to Nadi. They spent a couple of romantic days at the Sofitel, making love as often as their bodies would allow.

Hannah was acting nervous on their last night together. "Remember that you asked me what the medicine man said to me that day?"

"Yes." Robert responded.

"Well, I have something to tell you." Robert listened intently. "I'm pregnant."

Robert was confused. "What did this have to do with the medicine man?"

"He could tell by looking at me that I was pregnant."

Robert was silent.

"It happened when you came to Staunton for my father's service. Remember it was the only time that we didn't use protection."

Robert still needed to hear that there was no chance that this was Jack's baby.

"I figure that makes me about two months along. I haven't seen Jack in four months. Robert, the baby is yours."

A little stunned, Robert grabbed her and hugged her. He loved her and had always wanted children. This was wonderful news.

"Hannah, you expect me to leave tomorrow knowing that you are carrying my child? That's not right. Is there any way that we could get married before I leave? I would feel better knowing that we are a family before I go."

"Let's go ask at the front desk." Hannah responded.

The man at the front desk was most cooperative. He picked up the phone and within five minutes a Lutheran Minister appeared. He was carrying all of the necessary paperwork.

"That was fast." Robert commented. He started to break out in a sweat. This was a lot for him to take in: a baby and a wife all within 20 minutes!

"Would you like to have the ceremony on the beach?" Hannah and Robert looked at one another and nodded, then they both started to laugh as the absurdity of the situation started to hit them both at the same time. The minister ignored their laughter and asked them to sign the papers. The three headed for the beach with the front desk attendant in tow as a witness. Ten minutes later they were married. Robert grabbed Hannah's face with both hands and kissed her as hard as he could. He said, "I love you so much." Hannah cried softly.

Chapter 24

The symptoms of arsenic poisoning are very similar to cholera.

The two held hands and walked down the beach after the ceremony. "Well Mrs. Graham, how does this all feel to you? How do you like having a family?" Robert asked grinning from ear to ear.

"You sure look happy." she commented, though she had the same smile on her face.

"This is pretty big," he said.

"Huge." Hannah responded.

They discussed their hopes and dreams for the future. Both of them wanted children. Hannah would return to Virginia in two months. They would have a big family wedding in Staunton, and then Hannah would move into Robert's place in Alexandria. They would have to look for a big house and she still wanted to finish her final year at Richmond. It would take some doing, but she wanted to finish her law degree.

"No regrets Mr. Graham?" she asked.

"Not one." he said. They stopped to look at the sunset and held one another in a long embrace. Robert leaned down to kiss her.

"I've never loved anyone as much as I love you Hannah."

"I love you like no other as well Robert."

"Let's have a wonderful life together," he said.

"That is the plan." she exclaimed.

Robert grabbed her hand and started to run down the beach back toward their hotel. Hannah giggled with delight and ran as fast as she could trying to keep up with him.

He picked her up and carried her through their hotel room doorway, carefully placing her on the bed. She pulled him down on top of her.

"Are you sure this is okay to do with the baby and everything?" he asked.

"Of course it is, silly. Come here," She said as she yanked him down on to the bed.

"Yes ma'am. Whatever you want."

Robert gingerly unzipped Hannah's dress and gently pulled it from her body. She smiled as she watched him. She was not so careful with his disrobing. Robert pulled Hannah up from the bed and led her to the shower. He started the water and waited for it to get warm before leading her inside. He soaped her body from head to toe and she returned the favor, locked in kiss as frequently as possible. They slid their soapy bodies together with Robert's large erection sandwiched between them. He grabbed his slippery penis and slid it up and down, all over her body, paying special attention to her swollen breasts. Robert was surprised to see how much Hannah's breasts had already reacted to the pregnancy. He was a breast man and was going to enjoy Hannah's breasts growing over the next seven months.

He wrapped her in a towel and carried her to bathroom counter, placing her gently on the white tile. She opened the towel and eagerly anticipated their union. Robert enthusiastically accepted the invitation, briefly fondling Hannah's large breasts before eagerly sliding himself between her open legs. Hannah's pleasure seemed to have increased with the pregnancy. Her orgasms were more numerous and intense than usual. Robert held out as long as he could before losing himself in full explosion. He wrapped his new bride back into her towel and carried her to the bed where they made love three more times that night knowing that this was the last time that they would be together for two months.

Robert's plane to Auckland was due to depart at 11A.M. Mike would be coming to get Hannah about the same time.

"This is crazy Hannah. You should be coming with me." Robert said.

"I know it's crazy, but this all happened so fast. We have the rest of our lives together."

"Okay, Mrs. Graham. I'm going to miss you. You come back safe to me."

"You got it, Mr. Graham."

Chapter 25

There are over 5,000 homicide poisonings in the United States each year.

Lori had been going crazy in Robert's absence. Something was not right and she was determined to figure out what it was. Robert had been acting differently and his sudden disappearance had her going out of her mind with curiosity. She dug through every file in his office and there was no record of any client that would have needed him to go out of town for a week. He had been so vague about where he was going. What in the world was he up to? Lori was losing her grip on him lately. He barely spent any time with her, and he certainly wasn't spending any money on her. She only had the week that he was gone to go through his office to find out what was happening.

She decided to go through all of Robert's personal finances while she was at it. She was most interested in his will and what he was leaving to her. He had told her that he was leaving her most everything after his divorce from Angela. She made copies of all of his financial statements including investments, credit cards, social security number, etc. She snagged some checks from various money market accounts. Still there was no record of where he went, whom he might be with and why. She couldn't just let him slip through her fingers. She had always had him just where she wanted him and she was dead set on keeping it that way.

She had gone through the office with a fine-toothed comb...nothing. She had to do the same with his house, there just had to be something there. There were still two days left before Robert's return. She started in his home office. The will was there and everything was in order the way he said it would be. The estate was to be equally divided between Lori and Robert's two sisters. She made copies of everything. The home office turned up nothing about his trip.

Lori ransacked the entire house, one room at a time. Robert was neat and organized. All of the paperwork had been in the filing cabinets. He always made hard copies of everything. Nothing unusual came up anywhere else in the house. She had even checked his phone records and credit card statements. Nothing. If he were truly seeing a client as he said he was, then there would be records backing it up. What was the big mystery? What was Robert hiding?

Lori decided to reward herself for her hard work. She took one of Robert's credit cards and headed to Dillard's for a little shopping spree. She called "the boys" on the way and asked them to meet her at Geranio for dinner, her treat. Robert would be home soon and she would get to the bottom of things, get him back under her control. She hadn't been paying attention before; now she was.

Chapter 26

Accidental poisonings are the fourth leading cause of death in children under the age of five.

Hannah was as happy as she had ever been. She was married to her one true love and they had a child on the way. She was cherishing her time on the island. She only had two months left and was determined to make the most of it. Her life was about to change drastically. This would be the last freedom that she would know for a long time. She would enjoy the time that she had left on the island and she would relish every moment.

She used her time riding in the mornings with Samu to concentrate on how to handle the situation with Jack. She did not want to hurt him, and he had a right to know the truth as soon as possible. She knew that the news needed to be delivered in person. After a week of thinking about how best to deal with the problem, Hannah sent a text to Jack asking him to meet her in Nadi the following week. He returned her text and agreed to meet her.

The two arranged to meet in the bar. Hannah embraced him the moment she saw him. This was going to more difficult than she had thought. She truly cared for Jack and had no desire to hurt him. Jack ordered two Australian Chardonnays. Hannah quickly changed her order to club soda. Jack gave her a quizzical look; she had always enjoyed a good glass of wine.

"Let me explain Jack."

"No, Hannah, I need to interrupt first. I have something that I need to say. This isn't easy for me, but here it goes."

Jack took a deep breath, and then started. "Hannah, I've met someone. I didn't plan it. It happened just after I saw you last. She's a local girl, a Fijian. I've never felt like this before. We are engaged and she's going to have my baby. I'm sorry Hannah, I never meant to hurt you."

Jack was so engrossed in what he was saying that he hadn't bothered to look at Hannah. He was shocked to see that tears were rolling down her cheeks, tears of laughter. "Hannah, are you really laughing? That's not exactly the reaction that I was expecting!"

Hannah tried to compose herself. "Let me clarify. I came here to tell you the same thing, Jack."

She explained the entire story to Jack, all about Robert, the funeral, everything.

"So you mean to tell me that you are now married and pregnant? That's a lot to take in!" Jack burst into laughter.

"That's pretty funny isn't it?"

"Hilarious!" The two couldn't stop laughing. "How bizarre is it that we both had the same thing happen at the same time?" They raised their glasses for a toast.

They ordered dinner and enjoyed the evening as two old friends. It was a bittersweet evening for both of them. After dinner they took a walk on the beach. Jack had a million questions for Hannah. What were her plans, where would she be living, when would she finish law school? Hannah had very few answers. She explained to Jack that these things would unfold as she returned to life back in Virginia. Jack walked Hannah back to her room and hugged her tightly, knowing that he might never see her again. Jack was gone by the time Hannah woke up in the morning.

Mike arrived-mid morning to pick up Hannah and bring her back to the island. Hannah was sad about losing Jack from her life, but knew that she had done the right thing. She had much to look forward to in her new life. She only had several weeks left in Fiji and she was going to make the most of what time she had left.

Chapter 27

In the 1570's over 30,000 people were believed to be involved in poisonings in Paris.

Robert returned home to a defiant and angry Lori. She demanded to know where the hell he had been and what he had been up to. She did not like what she saw in him. He looked relaxed, tan, and, worst of all, happy. This was not going to be good, she just knew it.

Robert had thought about how to deal with Lori on the long plane ride home. He concluded that he would divulge his marriage and the pregnancy to Lori. There was no reason to hide it from her; there was nothing that she could do now that they were married with a baby on the way. She would just have to accept it or he would have to fire her.

"Hannah and I are married and," he continued, "we are having a baby."

All of the blood drained from Lori's face and her expression changed from anger to rage. Her mind raced as she processed this new information as quickly as possible without giving herself away. Robert studied her face and waited for a response.

Lori composed herself and swiftly grabbed Robert to extend a congratulatory hug. "Oh, Robert, I am so thrilled for you. When did all of his happen? Please tell me everything." Robert was more than eager to tell anyone who would listen about Hannah and the baby. He was beaming. Lori listened to every detail, hoping that there would be some bit of information that she would be able to use against them.

Lori asked Robert about their plans. He told her that they really hadn't discussed any plans past Hannah finishing up her time in Fiji and then moving in with Robert upon her return.

Lori's mind raced as she processed so much new information. She kept telling herself that there would be a way to make this work to her advantage…somehow. Robert babbled on for what seemed like forever to Lori. She congratulated him again and offered to help if there was anything that she could do for the happy couple.

Lori excused herself early from work that day telling Robert that she wasn't feeling well. The truth was that she had to go home and plot, regroup; figure out where to go from here. She had counted on Robert to support her financially; this was a big fly in the ointment!

Lori spent a couple of hours alone in her apartment thinking about what to do next and finally came up with a solution.

It was time to celebrate. She called Josh and the boys and asked them to meet her for dinner and drinks, her treat, or more accurately her treat on Robert's credit card!

Lori returned to work the following morning with a new attitude. She was happy and cheerful, offering Robert any help that he might need in preparation for Hannah's return and the baby's birth. Lori really did seem to have turned her self around, so Robert agreed to take her up on her offer.

"We are going to need a house to start with, a big one with lots of bedrooms. We are going to have lots of kids."

Lori was on top of it, the following day she had several appointments lined up for them to look at houses. Robert was impressed. It only took a week to find the perfect house, in Arlington. Lori took care of everything. She arranged to have all of their things moved and personally shopped for furniture and accessories that they were lacking. Robert didn't have to lift a finger.

Robert had been writing to Hannah about Lori's miraculous turn around and how helpful and supportive she was being. Hannah was skeptical as she read the letters. Her intuition told her that something wasn't quite right here. She would give Lori the benefit of the doubt, for now anyway.

Chapter 28

Spain had several failed attempts at disposing of Queen Elizabeth of England by poisoning.

Robert told Lori how impressed he was with her change of attitude and how thankful he was for all of her help.

"Robert, I am so sorry for the way that I have behaved in the past. I guess I was jealous of you and Lori. Now I want to be part of your lives, part of the baby's life. I will do anything that it takes to make up for my past behavior," she said.

Robert was thrilled to hear her words. He had always liked Lori, but had found here recent behavior most unacceptable. They had a clean slate now, and life was good, really good for Robert.

"I want to cook you a special dinner tonight, Robert, to celebrate your marriage and the pregnancy. What would you like? I will make anything you want."

"I've always loved your Indian food, Lori. That would be great. Thanks!"

Lori spent the day preparing food. She had purchased a couple bottles of Gewurztraminer to go with the meal. She knew how much Robert enjoyed the German wine with Indian food and Robert was impressed by Lori's efforts.

"This may be the last dinner that you and I ever have alone together, Robert. Things are never going to be the same."

"Oh, don't be silly, Lori. There will be plenty of opportunity in the future for you and me to continue our friendship."

They toasted to their friendship. Robert started to feel extremely tipsy.

"I'm sorry, Lori, but I think I need to lie down, I'm not feeling so good."

Lori helped Robert up the stairs to his bedroom. She helped him undress and get under the covers.

Robert woke up in the morning naked, with a naked Lori lying next to him. "Lori, what the hell are you doing in my bed? And where are your clothes? What the hell happened?" He was in a complete panic.

"Don't you remember, Robert? You weren't feeling well last night." Robert felt foggy headed.

"I remember not feeling well at the kitchen table, and that's it. I don't remember anything after that."

"I helped you up to bed and you weren't feeling well. I tried to comfort you and one thing led to another…"

"What? I don't remember a thing! Are you kidding? That doesn't make any sense. Oh my god, what have I done?"

"It's okay, Robert. Don't worry. Hannah doesn't ever need to know. It will never go further than the two of us, I promise. Let's just pretend that it never happened."

"Lori, you are being awfully calm and understanding. This is really bad, Lori, I mean, I'm a married man."

"It's our little secret, and it's forgotten," she said. "Now, let's get up and get working on the house. We have a lot to do."

Lori and Robert spent the weekends preparing the house for Hannah and the baby. They only had five weeks left until Hannah was due to come home from Fiji but the house was starting to look like a home. Robert put most of his energy into the backyard. He envisioned his children playing there, and he wanted it to be perfect. Lori had fully stocked the kitchen with everything the couple might need including anything that the baby would need. In just a matter of weeks, the house was fully transformed and ready for the small family to live in. The two celebrated by hosting a barbeque and inviting Josh and the boys.

Lori was in hog heaven, having all of the men whom she adored in one place, all to herself. Robert was pretty happy, himself. He could not wait to have Hannah there soon, to start his new life with her. Lori had prepared a huge spread of various pasta salads; green salads and baby back ribs. She made a batch of mojitos with the fresh mint from the back yard. The boys were playing croquet on Robert's newly planted lawn.

Lori noticed that Robert had been missing for some time, so she went to find him. She looked all over the house, but he was nowhere to be found. She called his name. No answer. She checked all of the bathrooms, and found Robert in a pile on the floor in one of them.

"Robert, oh my god! What's wrong?" Lori asked. Robert just groaned. He was curled in a ball in the middle of the bathroom floor, holding his stomach. His forehead was soaked in sweat. Lori immediately called to the boys to come and help. The group managed to get Robert to his bed where they were able to cover him with a blanket and place a cold washcloth on his forehead.

"We need to get you to a hospital." Lori said to Robert.

He just shook his head and moaned. "Just let me lie here," he said. "I must have some food poisoning. It will pass."

It went against everyone's better judgment, but they decided to follow Robert's wishes and not take him to the emergency room. The boys helped Lori clean up from the party, and left her to tend to Robert alone.

Lori loved taking care of Robert. He was totally dependent on her right now, just the way she liked it. She stayed up all night by his side, bringing him water and fresh washcloths and he was feeling much better by morning.

Robert thanked Lori profusely for taking care of him all night. "I probably would have died last night, Lori, if you hadn't found me. I can't thank you enough for staying up all night and making sure that I was all right," he said.

Lori beamed as Robert spoke. She liked nothing better than to hear praise from Robert. "I'm always here for you, Robert. You know that." she responded. "I'm just glad that you are all right now."

It took him a few days to fully recuperate, but he was good as new by the middle of the week, back in the office, working hard. He did not tell Hannah what had happened. She had enough to worry about.

Chapter 29

During the Elizabethan era women used a combination of vinegar, chalk and arsenic to lighten their skin and lessen wrinkles.

Hannah was enjoying her time on the island. The pregnancy was agreeing with her. She hadn't had a bit of morning sickness and was still up for her daily rides with Samu. The morning rides on the beach were breathtaking. The natives had taken her in and treated her as one of the family. Hannah knew that she would never experience another time like this in her life. She felt excitement for her life as it was on the island and excitement for the life that was about to unfold for her in Virginia. She had everything that she could ever dream of.

Hannah and Robert had broken the news to their families about the sudden marriage and impending birth. Hannah's mother was thrilled by the thought of new life in the family so soon after the death of Hannah's father. Everyone was supportive and genuinely happy for the couple. There were many questions posed to the couple about their plans, but they had very few answers. Robert had decided to keep the new house as a surprise for Hannah upon her return.

Robert had been busy making secret plans to meet Hannah in Fiji and take her on a month long honeymoon in Australia and New Zealand before returning back to Virginia to start their new life. He had every detail in place. This would be the trip of a lifetime for both of them.

It wasn't easy keeping secrets from Lori, she was in his life all day at work as well as entwined in his personal life. Robert did not want to take a chance again that Lori would act strange and interfere with his plans. Taking a month off from work would require Lori's cooperation, but he decided to wait until the very last minute to inform her of his plans.

Robert continued to have problems with his health. It was up and down. When he was sick, he was violently ill and then it would pass. He made an appointment with his general practitioner who sent him to the lab for a series of tests. Everyone was baffled.

Robert began to fear the worst. That he was developing some sort of degenerative disease, just as his life with Hannah and the baby was about to begin. Lori held things down at the office and continued to care for Robert on his bad days. He honestly did not know what he would do without her.

The days were drawing near to Robert's departure for Fiji. He decided that it was time to tell Lori, especially in case anything happened to him while he was away. Lori took the news extremely well. She told Robert how thrilled she was for Hannah and him.

She decided to throw Robert a lavish bachelor party before he left and once again invited all of the boys. Lori had decorated Robert's backyard with Chinese lanterns and portable waterfalls. The Asian theme gave the yard a very festive feel. There must have been 50 guests in all, mostly Robert's friends.

Robert collapsed in the middle of the party, doubled over in pain. Once again, the sweat poured from his forehead. This time Robert begged for an ambulance. Within ten minutes the paramedics were there checking Robert's vitals. He was quickly removed by gurney and taken to the closest hospital. Lori rode with Robert in the ambulance and, once again, the boys stayed behind to clean up. Everyone began to wonder if there was something seriously wrong with Robert. His illnesses were becoming more frequent and severe.

Chapter 30

Ketamine, rohypnol, and GHB are common date rape drugs.

The doctors monitored Robert for the next 48 hours in ICU. They came up empty handed. Robert was feeling better and was due to leave for Fiji the following day to surprise Hannah. The doctors wanted him to stay in the hospital for at least a week to run more tests but Robert refused.

On the third day, Robert checked himself out of the hospital and took a cab home to pack a bag and pick up his passport. He headed off to the airport without informing anyone. It wasn't until Robert was at his gate ready to board that he called Lori.

She was more than surprised to hear that Robert had left the hospital and was boarding a plane. She begged him not to go. He didn't listen to her, just gave her some instructions about clients and said that he would be in touch.

The following 16 hours on the plane were a blur to Robert, except for when he changed planes in Los Angeles. He had never been so exhausted in his entire life. He felt almost refreshed when he landed in Nadi. He checked into his hotel and slept for another 30 hours before meeting Mike at the dock to take him to see Hannah. He could not wait to see her and to start their new life together. Robert chatted away as Mike listened quietly on the ride to Moturiki.

The crowd had gathered to see who would be coming off of the plane. Robert could make out Hannah's blond hair and expanding waistline as the plane approached the dock. Robert grinned from ear to ear the moment he saw her. He knew that he did not want to spend his life without her. Mike disembarked with Robert following closely behind. Hannah grew sheet white when she saw who it was. She ran to him and threw her arms around his neck. "Robert, oh my god! What are you doing here?"

"I came to surprise you and to take you on a proper honeymoon."

Hannah threw her arms around his neck once more and squeezed him tightly.

Robert stepped back, "Let me take a look at you." he said. "Wow! You look wonderful!" As he placed both hands on her belly, Hannah beamed. Between her tan skin and the pregnancy, she was radiant.

"How are you feeling?" he asked.

"Wonderful," Hannah replied. "I've not had any problems, including morning sickness…nothing. The medicine man has been taking good care of me."

"It shows," Robert said. "You look incredible."

Hannah paused a moment and tilted her head sideways as she looked at Robert. "What's going on with you?" she asked. "You look awful! You're so pale and thin. How much weight have you lost?"

"I'll tell you the whole story later. Let's take a walk around the island," Robert replied.

Hannah had two days left on the island. That evening everyone got together and prepared a huge feast for Hannah and Robert. They had fresh lobster and tilapia, coconut, bananas and an array of homegrown vegetables. They even had a special kava ceremony for Robert and Hannah.

Hannah was feeling ambivalent. She loved her Fijian family and the island, but also loved Robert, the baby and the new life that they were starting.

After dinner, everyone started to question Robert and Hannah. Where were they going to live? What were their plans? Would there be a wedding?

One of the natives chimed in; "Let's have a real wedding for Robert and Hannah before they leave. We can ask the medicine man to perform the ceremony." Everyone loved the idea, especially Hannah. She was touched that the natives wanted to do this for them.

It was set. They would motor over to see the medicine man the following day and have the ceremony on the beach. What a perfect way to spend her last day, Hannah thought.

The next morning, Hannah took her last ride around the island with Samu. She didn't say a word, just took in the beautiful surroundings and hoped that one day she would be back to the island.

The natives had been busy while Hannah was on her ride. They had asked Samu to take her for a long ride so that they could prepare for the wedding. Everything had been loaded into several small boats by the time the two had returned from their ride. Hannah was instructed to get into one of the boats.

"But I need to change my clothes for the ceremony," she protested. She was told not to worry about that and to follow instructions.

All 50 natives, including Hannah and Robert, piled into boats and headed southeast to the medicine man's island. Once there, Hannah was escorted to a heavily wooded area with most of the women. The men took Robert to the medicine man's bure.

Hannah was shocked by what she saw in the woods. There were dozens of fresh flower leis, a bamboo contraption of some sort covered in flowers, and a beautiful native gown.

The women were thrilled to see the look of surprise and delight on Hannah's face. They quickly explained to Hannah all of the preparations that they had brought for her wedding.

The bamboo raft, known as a bili bili, is part of the traditional Fijian wedding ceremony. The bride is to sit in the center of the covered raft or throne and to be carried to the ceremony by two male warriors. The traditional Fijian wedding dress is called a tapa and is made of fibrous bark. The bark is covered with beautiful prints of native flowers in tan, brown and black. The flowers would be everywhere. Hannah was most pleased and touched by all of the trouble that the woman had gone to on her behalf.

Robert was busy with the men, having a kava ceremony before the wedding. He too had been given a traditional wedding costume to wear that was very similar to Hannah's. The men explained to Robert what would transpire during the ceremony. Robert felt a bit embarrassed that these strangers were being so hospitable to him, but he was grateful for their generosity and compassion.

The women all sang traditional Fijian songs as they helped Hannah to prepare for the ceremony. They helped her slip into the tapa and then covered her neck with several leis. They carried the bili bili to the water's edge and loaded Hannah on the platform. There was a seat in the center of the platform for the bride to ride comfortably to the ceremony.

Meanwhile, back at the medicine man's bure, the men were helping Robert to prepare for the ceremony as well. They showed him how to wear the male version of the tapa, two layers of the mulberry bark around his waist and several flower leis around his neck.

Robert felt a bit silly, as though he were wearing a dress for the first time. He chuckled to himself and embraced the hospitality of his new friends.

All were ready; it was time for the ceremony to begin. Everyone was singing. Robert and the men headed down to the beach. Two of the "warriors" walked over to the beach where Hannah and the women were waiting. The men gingerly placed the bili bili in the water and floated Hannah over to Robert's beach.

Hannah looked like a goddess, Robert thought, as he watched her come across the water. Hannah was beaming.

Robert's heart had never felt so full. He was overcome with emotion as he watched his beautiful bride and their unborn child. He thought to himself of what a fool he had been to be so closed off to the possibility of Hannah. He had almost missed this opportunity for true love and joyful, fulfilled life. He closed his eyes and said a quick prayer, thanking God for his happiness and good fortune.

The singing continued and the bili bili was beached. The warriors escorted Hannah to Robert's side. They turned to face the medicine man. He spoke in his native tongue, but one of the warriors instructed Robert and Hannah in English. The ceremony was short and sweet. The medicine man gave Hannah a slight wink as he spoke his words.

Hannah's head was reeling as she tried to comprehend all of the changes that were taking place in her life. She did not want to miss a moment of it. Everything in her life was delicious and perfect. She wanted to make time stand still. She was sure of her love for Robert and knew that they would have a good life together.

The two embraced, as instructed, and it was over. The crowd cheered and broke into song once again. Hannah cried as she hugged and thanked everyone for their generosity.

The reality of her leaving Fiji was beginning to sink in. Everyone was invited back to the medicine man's bure for an official kava wedding ceremony. Hannah knew that this would be her last kava ceremony and her last visit with the medicine man.

Chapter 31

Agatha Christie learned about the poisons that she wrote about when she worked in a hospital as a pharmacy dispenser.

The kava ceremony lasted for several hours. No one wanted it to end, but it was getting dark and time for everyone to head back to the island.

Hannah had dreaded this moment, saying goodbye to the medicine man. They both had tear filled eyes as they said their goodbyes. He hugged Hannah and wished her well, then placed his hands on her belly and blessed the baby inside. Robert and Hannah led the crowd to the beach and the waiting canoes. The singing recommenced and continued the entire way home.

The natives had one more surprise for the newlyweds. They had built a canopy on the beach for the honeymooners to have partial privacy for their wedding night. It was built with bamboo and sheer fabric covering it and was decorated with fragrant flowers.

Robert and Hannah were delighted by the canopy and thanked everyone once again for their thoughtfulness. They hugged everyone goodnight and were left alone on the beach.

"Well, Mrs. Graham," he said as he offered his hand to Hannah, "shall we step inside our honeymoon suite?"

"Of course, Mr. Graham. I would be delighted!" Hannah took Robert's hand as she grinned widely at him. Robert returned the grin.

The two stepped inside and lay down on the bedding that had been provided for them. Robert placed both hands on Hannah's swollen belly. "I love you both so much Hannah. Thank you for being my wife"

"You're welcome," she said. "Thank you for being my husband and giving me a family."

Robert placed both hands on Hannah's face and gingerly kissed her on the lips. He pulled back to take a better look at her. He looked into her eyes, smiled and then covered her face with little tiny kisses. Then he grabbed her as tightly as he could and gave her a big squeeze. Hannah let out a squeal of delight followed by a giggle. Robert let out an "mmmm, mmmm, mmmm" sound as he squeezed her.

It was a mutual agreement not to make love that night due to limited privacy. They would be alone the following night and every night thereafter for the rest of their lives. The couple slept soundly in warm embrace.

Chapter 32

Ingested acorns are considered toxic.

The heat of the sun woke the newlyweds very early. Breakfast was waiting for them. Hannah's host family had prepared a traditional Fijian breakfast for them consisting of scones and Bibinka, a traditional bread made from coconut, sugar, egg, cheese and the native cassava plant. The breads were accompanied by an array of native fruits. Hannah was used to the cuisine, but Robert was impressed. He had been living on bachelor food and this was heaven to him.

Hannah excused herself and returned to the kitchen wearing her traditional Fijian sulu. It made her sad to know that this was the last time that she would be wearing the outfit and the last time that she would be having a meal with her host family, but she quickly snapped out of her sadness once she reminded herself of her new life with Robert and their unborn child.

Robert changed into some shorts and a t-shirt. Mike was due to arrive at 10A.M. Robert had not filled Hannah in on the details of their honeymoon and she did not care. She knew that whatever Robert had planned for them would be wonderful. Hannah wrote out all of her contact information and gave it to her family, promising to keep in touch. They heard the roar of Mike's engine in the distance and knew that it was time to go.

Hannah contained her emotions as everyone walked to the pier to meet the plane. Everyone on the island was waiting to say goodbye to Hannah. She almost made it through the crowd until she came to Samu and then she lost it. "Thank you so much for all of the wonderful rides on the beach and for your friendship."

Samu responded. "It was such a pleasure, Miss Hannah. I expect to get letters from you every week."

"Of course," she said giving him a big hug.

Mike was waiting at the pier. He was all smiles as usual. The entire island escorted the couple to the pier for the final goodbye. Hannah had no idea where they were going, only that they wouldn't be back in Virginia for a month. Hannah remained composed as she said her final farewell. Before they knew it they were off and in a few short moments landed again on another island.

Hannah looked at Robert with surprise. "That's not Nadi. Where are we going?"

"It's a surprise. Just wait," he responded.

Hannah could see a large group waiting at the pier, mostly natives and a few Caucasians. There were a couple of men playing guitar and everyone was singing. They disembarked and each was handed a coconut with a beverage and straw in it. Several fresh flower leis were placed around their necks.

"Are we on Turtle Island?" Hannah asked.

Robert responded with a wide grin and a nod. "I've always heard about this place, but never dreamed that I would come here. Thank you, Robert. This is a dream come true!"

"You are welcome," he said, still grinning like a Cheshire cat. He found that pleasing Hannah made him feel good as well.

The staff of natives as well as the other guests on the island, mostly Australian couples, welcomed the two. Turtle Island only allowed children on the island at Christmas time. The staff invited the couple to sit while they asked them questions about their likes and dislikes as far as food, drink and activities went. They assured Hannah that a doctor was always on call at the infirmary should there be any concerns with the pregnancy.

The couple was escorted to their own private bure, a beautiful mostly bamboo cottage with a living room, bedroom and large bath. Hannah was thrilled with the accommodations after having lived so primitively for the past year. She couldn't wait to take a bath in the beautiful, large tub.

Hannah soaked for an hour. Robert left her alone except to bring her a tropical fruit drink. She thanked him and swiftly returned to closing her eyes and basking in the moment of a warm bubble bath. Robert wrapped her in a fresh towel as she stepped out of the tub. He was immediately aroused as he saw her newly voluptuous figure stepping out of the tub. He knew that he couldn't wait any longer.

Robert pulled Hannah towards him and wrapped his arms around her damp, swollen body. He kissed her as he allowed her towel to drop to the floor. He cupped her engorged breasts in his hands. "Hannah, my god, they're huge!" he exclaimed. Hannah giggled. Being six months pregnant suited her. The once athletic body was now more curvaceous and feminine.

Robert led her to the bed. The made love for the next hour, then fell asleep with the ceiling fan gently stirring overhead. The bell chiming that it was time for cocktails before dinner awakened them. Hannah and Robert dressed for dinner and headed over to meet the other island guests.

There were six other couples on the island, mostly from Australia. Hannah and Robert immediately liked one particular couple from Sydney, Joan and Ted. They were a bit older, but seemed to be full of fun. They sat together at dinner. The meal was spread out on white linen, good silver, candles, and all of the Australian wines that you could drink. It was a four-course meal fit for a king. They would soon learn that lobster was to be a part of each and every meal. The couples made plans to get together the following day.

Once inside their bure, Robert resumed just where they had left off earlier in the day. He eagerly removed Hannah's dress and quickly peeled off his shorts and dress shirt. They were back in the bed in no time. Hannah's body had become much more sensitive while pregnant. She found lovemaking to be more satisfying and wanted to make love much more frequently. Robert was happy with Hannah's newfound sensuality. They made love again for an hour before dozing off to sleep, Hannah wrapped tightly in Robert's arms.

Chapter 33

In early France the tomato was thought to be the toxic relative of the deadly belladonna. Once discovered to be edible, it was known as the love apple or pomme d'amour and was thought to be an aphrodisiac.

It was Hannah who woke Robert up at five in the morning. She was feeling amorous yet again. Robert was more than happy to oblige. Robert had signed up for an early morning fishing trip and was out the door by six o'clock. Hannah had signed up for a morning horseback ride and was able to go back to sleep for three more hours.

The two met for a late breakfast of lobster omelets, coconut pancakes and fresh fruit. They compared notes on their mornings and made plans with the staff for their afternoon activities. They opted for a private beach and a picnic on the other side of the island.

They returned to their bure, changed into swimsuits and headed back to the dock where the staff was waiting for them with a small motorboat and a picnic. They were dropped at their own private beach and were told that they would be picked up at four o'clock.

They promptly ditched their bathing suits and romped in the water naked, loving the feeling of the sun and the salt air against their bare bodies. It was the most relaxing afternoon that either of them could ever remember.

Hannah unpacked the picnic and couldn't believe her eyes; lobster, fresh baked goods, champagne, and sparking water – the works! After lunch, the two fell asleep on their blanket.

It was four o'clock before they knew it and the staff was returning to pick them up. They had plans with Joan and Ted for a six thirty sunset cruise. They had plenty of time for another love making session before heading off for their cruise. It had been a perfect day, they both concluded.

The staff was waiting in a large fishing boat at the dock. The four boarded the boat and headed out for a tour of some of the nearby local islands. The staff made mai tai's for everyone, a virgin for Hannah. They were back in time for yet another incredible dinner on the beach. Back in the bure, they made love again before dozing off to sleep.

The next two weeks followed in the same way. It was an amazing time on the island. They never wanted to leave.

Everyone on the island gathered to say goodbye and Mike was waiting at the pier with his seaplane, bare feet and all. The natives played their music, gave them leis and hugged them goodbye.

Once again they were back in the sky, Hannah not knowing where they were headed next. It was back to Nadi, and then a connecting flight to their destination. Hannah's only clue was that the flight would take four hours. She concluded that it had to be either Australia or New Zealand. Four hours later, they landed in Sydney.

They hailed a cab and headed directly to the Sydney Hilton. What a change from Fiji, Hannah thought. The hotel room was small and contemporary. Hannah felt as though she were back in civilization for the first time in a very long time.

"Robert, when did you have time to plan all of this? Everything has been so perfect. I can't thank you enough for this trip of a lifetime." Once again, Robert just beamed as Hannah sang his praises.

Hannah immediately drew a bath in the beautiful bathroom. They wasted no time in christening their new room before dinner. Hannah was glad that she was pregnant on this trip; she had never eaten so much good food in her life and felt that she would be looking pregnant even if she weren't already!

The two spent the next week playing tourist around Sydney, mostly walking around the city and shopping. Hannah loved the style of the women in Sydney. She found them to be cosmopolitan and sophisticated. They spent some time with Joan and Ted who owned a beautiful home right on the harbor. They owned a boat and escorted Hannah and Robert all over the harbor, taking them to their favorite spots. It was fun for Robert and Hannah to be with locals for a change and not have to be seeing the city through the eyes of tourists the entire time.

The week in Sydney came to a close and it was time for the final leg of the honeymoon. It was a three-hour flight from Sydney to Auckland; they had an additional three and a half hour drive.

Hannah was most surprised when they ended up in Rotorua. "What made you think of Rotorua?" she wondered.

"I thought it was the most quiet and relaxing place in New Zealand for you to completely unwind before heading back to the chaos of your new life in Virginia."

An enormous smile spread across Hannah's face. "You are so thoughtful Robert! Thank you!" She threw her arms around him and gave him a big hug. He just grinned.

Rotorua was extremely quiet. They took in a Maori show, but that was about it. They walked, read, ate and made love.

It was finally time to bring up the subject of their new lives at home. "So how do you see our future lives together?" Hannah asked.

"Big house, lots of kids and a dog running around. Just plain happy I guess."

"That sounds wonderful. We've never really talked much about the future. How many kids do you want?"

"I think four sounds good."

Hannah's eyes almost bugged out of her head. "Four? Really?"

"Yes, really."

"Wow, I'll have to give that some serious thought." She just smiled and shook her head.

"How do you see the rest of our lives Robert? Seriously, I never really thought about how this is all going to play out. I still want to finish law school…and travel. The baby and the marriage all just sort of happened. Where are we going to live? Your apartment isn't baby friendly!"

Robert sat quietly and smiled. He watched Hannah's expressions as she spoke. God, he loved her, he thought to himself. He wasn't even listening any more. He was just enjoying watching her.

"Robert, are you even listening?"

"Yes, of course I'm listening. Don't worry about anything, Hannah. We'll figure it all out when we get home. Now come over here and let's make love."

Hannah slid into his strong arms, feeling the warmth of his body. "I don't know how you can stand making love to me anymore. I'm looking most like a beached whale these days!"

"A most beautiful beached whale," Robert responded.

Chapter 34

Sherlock Holmes' toxic seven percent solution contained cocaine.

The month long honeymoon had come to its conclusion. It was time to head home and begin a new life. They had less than two months before the baby was due.

It was going to be a long flight back to Virginia, with a quick plane change in Honolulu. Hannah had no problem sleeping the entire time. She had been feeling good throughout the pregnancy, but needed lots of rest.

They arrived at Dulles airport in the middle of the night. Robert had booked a room at the nearby Hilton.

Hannah questioned him, "Why are we staying here? Your apartment is only 20 minutes away."

"I was just thinking about you. I thought you would want to rest and arrive home feeling relaxed."

"Once again, you are so thoughtful, Robert."

Robert grinned, knowing that he had a surprise planned for Hannah. He wanted her to see the new Arlington house in the daylight so that she could get the full effect.

This was the first night that they did not make love. Hannah was just too exhausted. Robert woke early and ordered room service. Hannah woke hours later and prepared one last bath for herself. She knew that Robert's apartment did not have any bathtubs.

Robert had been on the phone with Lori all morning, getting caught up on all that he had missed. He was going to have a lot of work to make up for! He wanted to make sure that Lori had made all of the arrangements for the house, that everything would be in proper order for Hannah's big surprise. Lori assured him that he didn't have a thing to worry about.

Robert told Lori to expect them about noon. Hannah was dressed, fed and relaxed by the time they left their hotel. They took a cab to Arlington and pulled up in front of large brick house, with a perfectly manicured lawn and purple rhododendrons everywhere. Robert was impressed. Lori had been busy.

"What are we doing here, Robert?" Hannah inquired. "I just want to go and settle into your apartment."

"This will only take a minute," he said. "Just humor me. Trust me, you are going to like this."

Robert instructed the driver to wait. He helped Hannah out of the cab and helped her as she waddled up the walkway to the front door. He rang the bell and Lori answered the door.

"What are you doing here?" Hannah was confused.

"Welcome to your new home, Hannah. I bought this for us…and our children."

Hannah was speechless. She walked through the front door, trying her best to absorb all of the new information that she just been given. Quickly, they walked past the living room, through the fully stocked kitchen and Lori led them out to the back yard through the kitchen sliding glass door.

The couple was in shock as they walked out the kitchen door to the back yard. There were some 200 or so people, balloons, streamers, canopies, a band, flowers, etc.

"What the hell?" Robert boomed looking directly at Lori.

"Surprise!" Lori chirped. "Welcome to your surprise welcome home and wedding!"

Robert and Hannah exchanged a look of disbelief. Their feeling of shock quickly transformed to delight.

The two gazed across the lawn, trying to comprehend the entirety of the situation. Everyone they knew was there: Hannah's family, Robert's family, their college roommates, and childhood friends. It was unbelievable! Lori must have worked day and night putting it all together.

The couple slowly made their way through the crowd, stopping to converse with each person. It was overwhelming. Hannah was introduced to Robert's family for the first time. They were thrilled to meet her and expressed their excitement about the baby. Hannah and Robert continued to exchange looks of disbelief and delight as they made their way through the crowd.

Robert pulled Lori aside the first chance he had. "What the hell, Lori? When do you do all of this? How did you get all of this done?"

Lori just smiled at him. "I just wanted to make up for my past mistakes. I want nothing but the best for you and Hannah. You know how much you both mean to me."

Robert hugged her the moment she was finished speaking. "Thank you, Lori. I mean that from the bottom of my heart."

Lori excused herself and went to find Hannah. "Come with me," she commanded.

Hannah did as she was told. Lori grabbed her by the hand and led her through the crowd to the master suite upstairs. There was a gorgeous white satin wedding gown laid out on the bed. There were hair and make-up people waiting with tools in hand and flower girls and bridesmaids running around in lavender satin gowns.

Hannah looked at Lori. "How did you do all of this? That's the gown that I would have picked, and the bridesmaid dresses, all in my favorite color... This is unbelievable!"

"I had to do something," Lori said "to make up for my past bad behavior. I just wanted to show you how much you and Robert mean to me." Hannah cried as she extended a big hug.

Lori said, "Enough of this. We'll have time for all of this later. We need to get you ready for your wedding!"

Hannah picked up the dress. "Lori, how did you know that I would love this dress?"

"You've been my best friend for years, remember? I know you. Now, go get dressed!" Hannah did as she was told.

Lori handed Hannah a long silk robe, "Now go put this on and we'll start with your hair and makeup."

Hannah stepped into her new master bathroom and changed into the robe. Her new bedroom was in chaos. People everywhere. She sat quietly in a chair and had her makeup done. She closed her eyes and tuned out all of the noise around her. She wanted to take in everything that was happening. It was all surreal and she didn't want to miss a thing!

The makeup was done and it was time for her hair. The stylist decided to put Hannah's hair in loose ringlets to accentuate her bare shoulders in her strapless dress. When she was finished, the look was complete and she was stunning!

Lori handed Hannah a silk pouch. In it were Hannah's white pearl necklace and large white baroque stud earrings. "How did you remember?" she asked Lori.

"I'm very detailed oriented, remember? Now let's put them on. The wedding starts in thirty minutes. We don't have much time."

Hannah put on her pearls then stepped into the bathroom to put on the appropriate undergarments for her dress. Once again, Lori thought ahead. Knowing that Hannah would need a strapless bra, but not knowing her size, she'd had to buy several. The third bra fit perfectly. Lori had remembered to buy a slip and beautiful satin shoes in Hannah's size. The last thing, she put on was the dress. It occurred to both women at that moment that there would be a rather big problem if the dress didn't fit. Fortunately it did.

They heard the music start in the back yard. Lori had hired a small group to play classical music. It was time.

Hannah was stunning in her white strapless satin gown, white strand of pearls, and loosely curled hair. Her hair had grown quite a bit on the island and still had streaks of highlights from the sun.

Lori handed her a bouquet of lilies with a purple satin bow. Hannah commented, "I don't know how you did it, Lori, lilies are my favorite!"

"I know." said Lori. "Now let's get going."

Lori escorted Hannah downstairs. They waited for Cannon's "Pachabel" to start playing before commencing the walk across the lawn. Several of Hannah's sorority sisters were there as bridesmaids, and a couple of her nieces as flower girls. Everyone was wearing purple satin dresses, except Lori. "Why aren't you one of my bridesmaids?" Hannah inquired.

"That's not my thing. I'd rather be behind the scenes." Lori extended a hug to Hannah. "Now, go. It's time to get married."

"Pachelbel" started and Hannah followed the flower girls and bridesmaids down the aisle covered by an awning layered with lilies. Robert and his groomsmen were waiting at the other side of the awning. Hannah was surprised to see her minister from Trinity Church in Staunton. Is there nothing that Lori did not think of? She wondered.

The ceremony was short and sweet. Both Hannah and Robert were teary-eyed. This was their third ceremony, but it felt to them like the first.

As soon as the ceremony was over, the back yard quickly transformed into party mode. Lori had gone all out on catering, music, etc. The bride and groom wasted no time in hitting the dance floor.

The couple took a break to mingle with the guests. Robert pulled Lori aside, "Lori, I can't thank you enough for all that you have done, but I have to ask you. How did you pay for all of this?"

"Both your family and Hannah's family insisted on paying for everything, including a brunch that they are hosting for everyone tomorrow in town."

"Wow, that's incredible, so thoughtful."

"Don't worry, you will have plenty of expenses. Everything that has been done around here having to do with the house has gone on your credit card. It's going to be a whopper!"

Robert chuckled and gave Lori a kiss on the cheek. "Thank you again, Lori."

The reception lasted until nine o'clock. It had been an incredible day. Now Hannah wanted a little time alone with her new husband to tour her new home. Everyone left, including Lori.

She instructed the couple to meet in the morning at 11:00 at the Market Street Bar and Grill for brunch and that everything would be cleaned up and out of the yard by the end of the day.

Chapter 35

A poisonous snake is still able in inject deadly venom up to an hour after it's death.

The couple breathed a sigh of relief as the last guest walked out of their new front door. They looked at one another with the same expression: a combination of joy and exhaustion. Robert put his arms around her and they hugged in the doorway for several moments.

"Come, let me show you around your new home, Mrs. Graham." Robert led her, room by room, through the six-bedroom house.

"My god Robert, there are so many bedrooms! Why?"

"One for us, one for each of our children and one guest room."

"Oh that's right. I forgot that you wanted four! Can we just start with one for now?"

The house was enormous and beautifully furnished. Robert and Lori had picked out some starter pieces, but had left most of the decision making for Hannah once she got settled in. She liked the feeling of lack of clutter. Hannah's favorite room was the expansive kitchen that connected to the open family room. "I love everything about this place Robert. It's all so wonderful, but can we go to bed now?"

Robert laughed and led her by the hand upstairs to the master suite. It was still in a somewhat disheveled state, but Lori had promised that it would all be cleaned up the following day.

Robert helped Hannah out of her gown, bra and underwear, he pulled the covers back and helped her into bed and then he joined her from the other side. He put his arms around her and gently kissed her ever so slowly. To both of their surprise, they were instantly aroused. Robert wasted no time in consummating their most recent marriage.

The two slept hard for the next eight hours and made love again before heading to meet everyone at the grill. They felt relaxed and refreshed as they entered the restaurant. It seemed that almost everyone was there who had been at the reception the night before. The restaurant was decorated with purple balloons; streamers and each table had an arrangement with Hannah's favorite lilies.

The guests stayed through most of the afternoon. Hannah and Robert were relaxed and content, enjoying the company of so many family and friends. They noticed that Lori was absent...odd they thought.

They returned to their new home about four o'clock. Lori was there. The place was immaculate. Lori had organized several cleanup crews to get the place back in shape in such a short time. Her organizational skills were impressive; she made it all seem like no big deal.

"Lori, you are something else. I can't believe what you've done." Robert commented.

"Amazing!" Hannah agreed.

"You two relax and get settled. I still have a few things to finish up."

It didn't take any convincing from them to relax. They were exhausted! They took a seat on the new oversized sofa in the family room. Hannah put her feet up on the coffee table. "This is heaven!" she said. "You did a great job of picking all of this furniture out. It's good looking and comfortable."

Lori came in to say goodbye. "It looks like everything is finished here. I just have one more thing. It's your wedding/house warming gift."

"Lori you have already done so much. Please, no gift."

"It's something that I want to do, for you two and your new life. I'll be right back."

Lori returned after a moment with a Golden Retriever puppy in her arms with a big red ribbon around its neck.

"Oh how adorable!" Hannah exclaimed and immediately took the puppy from Lori.

"What a great idea, Lori! Thank you," Robert added.

"What are we going to name him?" Hannah asked.

"We'll have to think about that," Robert responded.

"Well, you two have fun trying to figure that out. I'm out of here."

They walked Lori to the door and both gave her an enormous hug. "You are incredible. We will never be able to thank you enough," Robert said.

"I'll see you tomorrow morning at work." And with that she was gone.

The couple exchanged a look of relief. It was time for them to collapse, except that they now had an eight-week-old puppy to care for.

"Let's take him out back." Robert followed her.

"We need to call him something that's connected with Lori, since she gave him to us. I know, we can call him Lewis, just like her last name. It's kind of cute, actually." "All right, Hannah, it's a little weird, but that's his name."

Chapter 36

Acorns produce a toxic substance known as tannic acid.

It was back to work for Robert first thing Monday morning. He knew that he would be facing a mountain of work to make up for being gone an entire month. Lori was already at the office when he arrived. She had everything organized in order of priority for him. Lori handed him a cup of coffee and a stack of papers, then she started to fill him in on everything that he had missed.

Hannah had her hands full with the house. They only had two months until the baby was due. She decided to tackle one room at a time, the first being the baby's room. Hannah chose a yellow and blue motif. The puppy, Lewis, was a good companion for Hannah while Robert was logging extra hours at the office.

Hannah had dinner prepared for Robert every night when he dragged himself in late. He was exhausted, but wanted everything in the office caught up by the time that the baby arrived. The two were able to spend a relaxing couple of hours together each evening before heading to bed and making love.

Hannah was making great progress on the house. Little by little, it was coming along. Her Lamaze classes started and Robert was able to meet her once a week in the evening. Hannah's mom and brothers were around to help as much as possible. Everything was in order. They were ready for the baby's arrival.

Lori had been busy with Robert at the office and hadn't seen much of Hannah. Lori called and invited her to lunch one day to get caught up. She said she wanted to take her to a girl's fancy lunch, so they chose La Bergerie. They planned to meet on Saturday at noon.

The birth was less than a month away. Hannah was finding it difficult to find things to wear. She made a special trip to Apple Seed Maternity to find something pretty to wear to lunch. She found an adorable dress that worked. She loved being pregnant, but was looking forward to getting her old body back.

Saturday arrived and Robert dropped Hannah at the restaurant on his way to the office. Once inside, Hannah looked around and didn't see Lori anywhere. She walked to the back of the restaurant and was startled by a loud "surprise" shouted at her by a large crowd of women. She was completely surprised. Lori greeted her.

"Lori, did you do all of this?"

"Yes, with the help of your mom and Robert's mom. Now come, let's have some fun."

Lori had thought of every detail, as usual. She had games organized, and, of course, the room was decorated in the same colors as the baby's nursery, yellow and blue. There were balloons, streamers, flowers and baby booties everywhere. The 30 or so women roared with laughter as they played the games. The gift opening took several hours, as there were so many. Hannah was overwhelmed. This baby was going to have everything!

The afternoon wound down and Robert appeared with their Escalade to carry all of the gifts home in.

"So you were in on this?" she asked.

"Of course, all I had to do was keep quiet. Lori did the rest." The car was full to capacity. Hannah turned to thank Lori once again, for her thoughtfulness and all of her hard work.

"I'm going to be writing thank you notes for weeks, thanks to you!" The two women giggled.

"See you bright and early in the office tomorrow, boss."

"Yeah, thanks a lot." Robert mumbled.

Hannah talked endlessly on the way home. She was wound-up and excited by her party. Robert smiled as he listened to the details of the day. Robert looked at her as she spoke, lost in her beauty. I love this woman, he thought. I really love this woman and am so happy right now. Robert continued to smile as Hannah babbled on. She had no idea that he was not listening to a word she said.

They unloaded everything from the black Escalade into the nursery. It was going to take some work to find room for everything! Hannah went to change her clothes and plopped herself down on the sofa in the family room. Robert joined her. He began to rub her swollen feet. "Hannah, these are our last few days together, just the two of us. Life is about to change…drastically. How do you feel about the baby coming?"

"Our life is so perfect right now, Robert, I think that the baby will only make our life better. I have no misgivings. I do want to finish law school one day however."

"You will. I have no doubt."

Robert suggested that they go to bed early. Hannah agreed with a smile and followed him to the bedroom.

"I want to enjoy you with your wonderfully pregnant body. It will be gone soon."

"I must say that I have been enjoying it as well. My entire body has been so much more sensitive than usual."

"I've noticed," Robert said, with a big smile on his face.

His fingers gently traced the outline of her breasts, slowly circling her large nipple. They continued down to the soft skin of her belly. By the time his fingers made their way to her clitoris, she was fully engorged.

"Wow Hannah, you are ready!"

"Yes, I most certainly am!" Robert moved in behind Hannah. They had found, recently, that spooning was the most effective position for them. Robert was able to stimulate her breasts from this location. When they were finished, both fell asleep in this position and woke in the morning the same way.

Chapter 37

The toad produces a psychoactive drug that can be released by stroking the toad's chin.

The next couple of weeks were a flurry of activity. Robert was putting in long hours at the office and working in the back yard on his off time. It was fall and there were tons of leaves to be raked. Hannah was putting the final touches on the nursery. They had been through two months of nesting and they were ready.

Hannah was preparing breakfast one Monday morning when her water broke. She had Robert's undivided attention. "I guess it's time." She looked and him and laughed.

"It looks that way," he said looking mortified. "Do whatever you need to do. I'll meet you right here in 10 minutes."

Hannah nodded. Robert called the doctor and Lori, then grabbed the packed suitcase and put it in his Escalade. Hannah went upstairs to change her pants and brush her teeth. They were out the door in less than 10 minutes.

Robert drove calmly to the Inova Alexandria Hospital. Even with traffic, they were checking in at the front desk within 15 minutes. Both the doctor and Lori were already there and waiting. Hannah was escorted to her room via wheelchair. She was to give birth in her private room as long as there weren't any complications. The nurses swiftly hooked her up to several monitors to watch her vitals as well as the baby's. Everything looked good. The contractions were four minutes apart.

Dr. Lowenstein came to check Hannah vaginally; everything was looking on track. She should be giving birth within the next few hours. She agreed to have an epidural since there was still time. Robert and Lori were both in the room fully clothed in hospital gowns and masks. The rest of the family was beginning to gather in the waiting room. Lori had made sure to call everyone from both sides of the family. Lori had also remembered to bring the video camera.

Hannah did her best to try to rest through the contractions. Two hours later, Dr. Lowenstein came in and told her that it was time to push. 20 minutes later, a little head with brown hair made its way into the world, a boy. They had already decided to call him Charles or Charley for after Hannah's father. Lori had taped the entire event and was the third person to hold her new godson.

Charley was checked out and cleaned up, then given back to his mother to breast-feed. It was a natural connection. The two rested comfortably together for several hours. A nurse came in and gave Hannah some simple instructions and they were discharged. Never in a million years did Hannah think that when she got up that morning, she would be going home with her new son that afternoon!

Lori had already excused herself to run over to the Grahams' house before they got home. She wanted to let Lewis out and have the foyer filled with balloons and flowers. It was a very nice welcome home for the little family. Lori offered to hang around, prepare food, answer the phone and entertain anyone who might stop by to see the baby. The couple readily took her up on the offer.

Lori stayed in the guest room for the next several days, helping in any way that she could. She and Robert were working out of his home office. She prepared trays and brought them to Hannah so that she and Charley could have undisturbed bonding time. Robert was hands on with the baby, changing diapers and rocking him to sleep.

After four days, Lori went back to her apartment and the Grahams developed a new routine in their lives. Charley was a low maintenance baby and slept through most of the night. The Grahams were so pleased with their new life and the addition of Charley to their family.

Lori was around a lot, offering to help in any way that should could. She babysat frequently so that the couple could go out on dates.

One night, while out alone at dinner, Hannah said, "Robert I've been thinking. Lori has done so much for us, I think it's time that we do something for her. She has no personal life to speak of and no family…we are it for her. Why don't we send her on a nice vacation somewhere?"

"I think that's a wonderful idea Hannah. Do you have any ideas where?"

"No, but I'll think about it. Let me know what kind of budget to stay in and I'll make all of the arrangements, okay?"

"Okay." They toasted to Lori's vacation.

Hannah did her research over the next few days and decided to purchase a weeklong cruise in the Caribbean. They presented the gift to Lori that week when she came over for dinner. The expression on her face was more of shock than surprise.

"You guys are incredible. No one has ever done anything like this for me before. I don't know what to say."

"You're welcome," they replied in unison.

"Now, pick a week and go!" Robert ordered.

"Okay, boss, I will." Two weeks later Lori was sailing around the Caribbean Islands.

Chapter 38

Absinthe, an alcoholic liqueur made of wine and wormwood, has toxic effects and is a striking green color.

Hannah took naturally to motherhood, but did not want to let her dreams of finishing law school go by the wayside. She decided to take some online classes to keep her education going. She and Robert were both training for a marathon. Their lives were full and happy.

When Charley was six months old Hannah suspected that she might be pregnant. She broached the subject with Robert. He was thrilled. She made a trip to see Dr. Lowenstein and he confirmed her theory. Hannah was a bit dumbfounded. They had been using birth control. She concluded that they were just incredibly fertile together.

Lori was a constant figure in their lives, frequently at the house, helping with the baby. She seemed shocked about the news of another pregnancy as well, but made no comment. Hannah did her best to keep up with Charley and her classes, but the marathons had to go. The pregnancy made it much too taxing.

Robert and Hannah had their regular dates. Hannah made a point of dressing for each date, feeling sexy and proud of her looks. Robert found her to be more beautiful with each day. They enjoyed each other's company, rarely got short with one another and enjoyed the same things. Their sex life was always improving and changing: both eager to try new things to please one another. Robert's impatience and passion had tempered somewhat over the years and he was spending more time exploring the world of foreplay with his wife. Life was very, very good.

Baby Valerie was born when Charley was a year and a half. Blond hair, brown eyes, she was named after Hannah's grandmother. She was a wonderful addition to the family. Lewis was very patient with the babies, allowing them to pull on his tail and stick their fingers in his mouth.

The little family planned many outings together. Lori was almost always included. She was a huge help to Hannah with the children, not to mention everything that she did for Robert in the office. They felt as though she were a family member and were happy to have her around. She made sure never to overstay her welcome.

The five of them took a trip together to the Outer Banks in North Carolina. They rented a huge home and took long walks on the beach while Robert went fishing.

Lori and Hannah had many long talks. Lori revealed a side of her life that she had kept private her whole life. "I don't think that anyone truly likes me. That's why I always have to do things for people; otherwise they won't like me. The parties, the decorating, helping, it's all to please everyone. No one could ever like me for me. My father told me that over and over again when I was a child."

"Don't be ridiculous, Lori. Robert and I love you for you, not because of what you do for us."

"That sounds nice, Hannah, but hard to believe."

"Maybe you need to talk to a therapist. It sounds like your dad did some pretty serious damage to your self-esteem."

"Yes, I'm sure you're right. I don't want to go to a therapist. Let's change the subject."

Hannah thought she had been given some insight into Lori for the first time and was disappointed that Lori chose not to explore her situation to improve it. At least, Hannah felt that at she had a better understanding of Lori now. She later shared the conversation with Robert.

"Oh, I don't believe that Lori has low self-esteem. She just likes to help people." Hannah was a little disappointed that Robert wasn't even listening.

Several weeks after returning home from the Outer Banks, Hannah realized, once again, that she was with child. She had to laugh. They had been on birth control the entire time. Little Alexa was born seven and a half months later. They named her after Lori – Loreen Alexandra Lewis. Alexa had blond hair and brown eyes just like her older sister.

Chapter 39

Vincent Van Gogh died from drinking absinthe.

The couple had their hands full with three children all under the age of five! They were fortunate to have lots of help. Lori was always around and so were Hannah's mom and siblings. Robert's family came whenever they could. The house was full of noise and love.

Robert had installed quite a play area in the massive backyard. The children had a slide and swings. It was a great place for them to play with Lewis as well. He kept the children very well entertained.

They took as many family trips as possible before any of the children started school and they would no longer be able to go. They rented the same house in the Outer Banks, on the beach in Rodanthe. They went to Disneyworld, Virginia Beach and the Blue Ridge Mountains in the fall then rented a house on the beach in Islamorada and spent a long weekend furniture shopping in High Point.

When at home, the family spent their time riding bicycles (children in tow), kayaking and hiking. Both Robert and Hannah still managed to get a run in almost every day, though training for marathons was out of the question. Hannah's studies were also out of the question with three toddlers in the house. She was determined to complete her studies, but it would have to wait until the children were all in school.

The family decided on one last trip before Charley started the first grade. Rodanthe was the family favorite. They had two relaxing weeks and Lori tagged along.

With Lori around, Robert and Hannah were able to steal away for some romantic time together, long walks on the beach and quiet dinners for two.

"So, Hannah, are you happy?" Robert caught her off guard with the question at dinner one evening.

"Of course! Why do you ask?"

"Because we are living the dream. This is the best life I could ever imagine. You, the kids and me...even Lewis is the best dog ever! I just want to make sure that you don't have any regrets. You could have had a life with Jack and traveled the world. That was your dream. You're a mother in the suburbs with three kids, not exactly what you had in mind, Hannah."

"Honestly, I can't imagine being any happier, Robert. Our life is a perfect. I wouldn't change a thing. It's been wonderful. I have no regrets, not one."

Robert reached across the table to hold Hannah's hand as he looked at her and smiled. She returned the look.

The vacation ended all too quickly. It was time for school to begin...the first of many back to school days. Charley was excited to be away from home and away from his sisters.

It was on the first day of school that Hannah realized she was yet again with child. She broke the news to Robert that night in bed. He was thrilled, of course.

"Okay, Robert. Now you have the four that you wanted. Can we be done? Birth control has not worked for us. At this rate we are going to end up with a dozen children. Will you please consider a vasectomy?"

"I've never thought about it before, but I promise to give it some serious consideration. Obviously, we have to do something!"

They made love that night. The lovemaking had grown more intimate over time; it was gentle and sweet at times, erotic at others. There was no boredom in the Graham bedroom!

The school year flew by quickly with the family spending more time taking weekend trips now that Charley was in school.

They decided to buy a second home on Smith Mountain Lake for boating, kayaking, fishing, etc. They made the four and a half hour drive to the lake house at least once a month. The house was large enough for all of the kids, plus guests.

Robert surprised everyone by purchasing a speedboat. When the kids were a little older, he wanted them to take up waterskiing.

The house was a great addition to their lives. Everyone enjoyed their time on the lake. Lori tagged along most of the time, which pleased both Hannah and Robert since her presence afforded them some alone time together.

Baby Virginia was born in the spring...blond hair and brown eyes just like her older sisters. They decided to call her Ginny. Hannah needed more help than ever with four children all under the age of six! Lori was always around providing any kind of help that Hannah needed. Lori was doing tons of carpooling for the Grahams. Hannah had an idea and presented it to Robert.

"Lori does so much for us and takes our kids everywhere. I think she needs a bigger car and I think that buying her one would be the least we could do, since she does so much for us."

"That's a great idea, Hannah. Why don't we give her the Escalade and we will get something a little bigger."

"Done."

The following week, they had the car detailed and presented it to Lori when she was at the house for a barbeque. Her Toyota was old and Lori had not taken good care of it. She seemed thrilled and surprised by the new vehicle.

Chapter 40

The odds of dying from a snakebite are one in thirty-six million.

Hannah received a surprise phone call one day while she was home alone with the kids. It was Josh.

"Wow stranger, I haven't talked to you in ages. How are you? Hannah asked.

"Things are good. I was hoping to have lunch with you sometime and get caught up."

"I guess we do have some catching up to do, Josh. I've had four children since the last time I saw you!" They talked for a few minutes and arranged to have lunch the following week.

Hannah relayed the conversation to Robert when he got home from work. "Hannah, I never told you that Josh was the one who sent me the article about your father's death. We have him to thank for our being together now."

"I had no idea! I'll have to thank him when I see him."

"Thank him for me too while you're at it!"

Josh was waiting at Asia Bistro when Hannah arrived. Hannah was taken back by his appearance. He had lost weight and naturally looked older than the last time that she saw him. Hannah had changed a bit herself. No longer the sweet looking college student, she had developed into a voluptuous beauty. Her body had more curves and her face more character. She was stunning in her own right.

Josh's face lit up the moment he saw her. He stood and greeted her with a kiss on the cheek.

"It's so wonderful to see you, Hannah."

"You as well, Josh. It's been way too long."

Hannah started the conversation by sharing with him what Robert had said about his being responsible for their getting together.

Josh chuckled "I guess you're right." They chatted away, getting caught up on the past six years since they had seen one another. When the food arrived, Josh changed the subject. His tone became serious.

"Hannah, I have something to tell you. I've thought long and hard about this, but I've decided that it's something that you just need to know, so here goes." Hannah didn't know what to expect, but she had a feeling in the pit of her stomach that it wasn't going to be good. "I know for a fact that Lori has been stealing from you and Robert for years, lots and lots of money, thousands and thousands. She has become quite bold about it lately and has even been bragging about it. She really despises you, Hannah, hates your guts actually. As far as she is concerned, you have everything that she was entitled to. You should have heard her complain about you two when you gave her a hand-me-down car. She was livid! She wishes you harm. Do yourself a favor. Hire someone to go through your books with a fine-toothed comb. Get your evidence, then confront her."

Hannah felt numb. She thought she would be sick. "I don't understand any of this, Josh. She is part of our family, my son's godmother. We named our dog and one of our daughters after her. How could this be?"

"I don't know, Hannah. She seems pretty messed up to me."

"Just do yourself a favor and hire someone, quickly, before she takes more of what is yours. Please do me a favor and give this to Robert. He'll know what it is."

Hannah gave him a quizzical look and shrugged "I don't know whether to thank you or punch you, Josh."

"I'm sorry, Hannah, you had to know."

Hannah lost her appetite. They chatted a bit, but Hannah's head was reeling. She was unable to focus.

"I'll let you know what happens. You are a good man." She kissed him on the check and was gone.

Hannah was in shock; she couldn't think straight. She went over and over what Josh had said in her mind. It didn't make any sense, and she didn't want to believe it. There just had to be some other explanation, she thought. Maybe Josh had it out for Lori and was making the whole thing up. She needed to talk to Robert right away.

Hannah arranged to have a babysitter take the kids to the park so that she could speak with Robert in private. The house was empty except for Hannah when he got home.

"Where are the kids?"

"They are with the babysitter. We need to talk."

"Is something wrong?"

"Yes, I'm afraid so."

Robert looked scared as Hannah spoke. "I had lunch with Josh today, and he gave me some very disturbing information."

"What?"

"It's about Lori. He claims that she has been stealing from us for years, lots and lots."

It wasn't sinking in to Robert's head. "She wouldn't steal from us. She is paid well, we buy her cars, give her vacations…no way. I don't believe it."

"Josh says we need to hire someone right away to go through the books. Robert, we have to do it, to know for sure. Oh, and he asked me to give you this." She handed him the envelope.

"What's this?"

"I don't know; he just asked me to give it to you."

Robert placed the envelope on the table. "I don't see how it could hurt to have an audit, but we don't want Lori to know what we are up to. I'll make a couple of phone calls. I'll be back."

Robert returned 15 minutes later. "We are all set. I'm meeting with a guy tomorrow. It's a start."

"I don't like this whole thing, Robert. It's making me sick."

Robert put his arms around her. "It's all going to be okay, Hannah. Don't worry."

"How are we going to act normal around Lori from now on?"

"I don't know, but we will."

Robert had almost forgotten about the envelope. He opened it. There was a hand written note from Josh and a photograph. Robert's face turned sheet white, he quickly sat to read the note, his heart was about to pound out of his chest.

Robert,

I should have told you this a long time ago. I've been feeling very guilty about not telling you. Please forgive me. The night that you and Lori ended up in bed together was all a lie. She gave you a ruffee that night and staged the whole thing. She wanted to have something to hold over your head in case you cut her out of your will. Nothing ever happened between the two of you. Enclosed is the picture that she took to blackmail you. Once again, I'm sorry for not telling you sooner. I hope that you can forgive me.

Josh

Robert looked at the photograph and gasped. It was of him and Lori nude in bed together. It was blown up enough to see the date on the People magazine lying on the bed. She wanted to make sure that Hannah would know exactly when the event had taken place… after their first wedding.

"That bitch! What an evil bitch! I can't believe it!" He now had Hannah's full attention.

"What is it, Robert? You look awful. What happened?" Robert handed her the letter. She read it. "I don't understand. What is this all about?"

"Hannah, I'm so sorry. I will try and explain."

He told her the whole story from the beginning. "Why didn't you ever tell me about this? I would have believed your version. You had no idea what happened."

"I just couldn't take the chance of losing you, Hannah. I'm so sorry."

"Are there any other lies between us?"

"No, absolutely not."

"I won't let her damage our marriage Robert. That's exactly what she wants. I can't get over what a twisted, sick person she is."

"Robert, I just remembered something else!"

"Now what? Do I even want to know?" he asked.

"When you were married to Angela and she cheated on you, Lori told me all about it, I mean every last little detail."

"Are you shitting me? She told you everything?"

"Yes, everything! I didn't have the heart to tell you. I wanted to protect you. I didn't want you to know that your best friend was betraying you."

"Ugh!" was all that Robert could utter. "And you still wanted to date me after knowing all of that?"

"Of course, Robert. I would never judge you based on something that Lori had said about you. I knew the real you from our first date. I knew in my heart who you were and what you were all about." Robert just listened with his eyes fixated on Hannah's face.

Things seemed normal on the outside over the next few days, but Hannah and Robert were anxiously awaiting some kind of response from the bookkeeper. On the third day he gave Robert a call. "From the bank and credit card statements you've given me, it looks like you have a big problem. I want access to all of your records to really do a thorough job. I need to get into your computer, your files, everything." Robert assured him that he would arrange full access for him. He needed to somehow get Lori out of the office.

He discussed the situation with Hannah. "Let's send her on another vacation. She would never suspect a thing."

"Great idea, Hannah."

"I'll book something for her tomorrow for a trip next week. That will work, won't it?"

"Sounds great, I'll call the bookkeeper."

The couple presented Lori with an envelope at dinner the following day: a week in Aruba.

"You guys are so wonderful! Thank you so much." Lori was thrilled and didn't seem to suspect a thing. It made the couple sick just to see her, but they had to play along, at least for now.

Chapter 41

Cleopatra died from a snakebite.

The bookkeeper arrived at Robert's office Monday morning with several assistants. They went through every file, computer, and receipt, anything that they could find. It took two days, but the consensus was that the Grahams had been taken for somewhere in the neighborhood of $120,000.

"She was getting sloppy recently. It wasn't hard to figure out. I suggest that you get the police involved, and I wouldn't waste any time if I were you."

Wednesday morning Hannah arranged for a babysitter. She and Robert went to the police station to file a formal complaint. They spent three hours filling out paper work. The police requested access to Robert's files. They would be in his office first thing Thursday morning to start their investigation. Robert and Hannah stopped to have a quiet lunch together on the way home.

"I'm exhausted, Robert. How are you feeling about all of this?"

"Betrayed, disappointed. It's still difficult to accept that she could be so calculating and ruthless."

"I agree. The whole thing makes me sick every time I think about it."

"I'm going to have to fire her the moment she gets back from Aruba. The shit is going to hit the fan, big time! It's probably going to get ugly."

"Life is never going to be the same." They ate their lunch in silence, contemplating the enormity of what was to come.

The Grahams made it through the weekend, dreading the confrontation that was coming on Monday morning. Lori arrived at the office, tanned and rested. Robert called her into his office first thing. "I'm sorry, Lori, but it's come to my attention that you have been stealing and I'm going to have to let you go."

Her face turned beet red. "Excuse me? You are what? And you are accusing me of what? You are going to pay dearly for this! I have done everything for you and your stupid little family. You've just made a huge mistake!" She stormed out, stopping at her desk to remove some things. She noticed that her drawers had been emptied.

Robert stood in the doorway. "The police have already confiscated your files."

She shot him an evil glare and was gone.

Robert called Hannah, "Well it's done, and it wasn't pretty. Hannah, I'm so worn out by all of this. I was thinking, how would you feel if I closed the office for a week and we take the kids and just hang out at the lake?"

"That sounds like heaven!" Hannah had the car loaded by the time Robert got home.

They decided not to tell anyone about the situation with Lori. Bad news travels fast enough they concluded.

The police were in touch with Robert several times a day, asking questions, wanting more information. They called Wednesday evening to let him know that Lori had been arrested. They had more than enough evidence to hold her. There would be a trial. Robert's stomach was in knots as the detective spoke.

He updated Hannah on the conversation. "I wish I could wake up and this would all be gone, just a bad dream. How is this all going to play out? I can't even imagine."

The situation with Lori was bringing the couple even closer together. Their little family was more bonded together than ever. The two relaxed as much as they possibly could at the lake, taking long walks, holding hands and sitting at the water's edge. They needed this time to regroup and prepare for whatever was coming their way.

Chapter 42

The bee is responsible for more deaths worldwide than any other insect.

Lori confessed everything to the police once confronted. She was immediately taken to jail where she awaited trial. Lori's entire family showed up at the trial. Her father was a successful attorney, but offered no legal or financial assistance to his daughter. She was given a court appointed attorney.

Hannah's testimony was the longest, and the most emotional. She read a letter to the court describing the close relationship that she had had with Lori over the past dozen or so years. She depicted her as a trusted member of the family, aunt to all of her children, implicit unconditional love.

The judge gave her the maximum sentence, two years. It was an emotional response in the courtroom. Lori was lead away.

Hannah felt weird thinking that they might never see her again. Robert put his arms around Hannah. "No one can harm us now. It's all behind us."

The Graham family settled back into a routine with the absence of Lori Lewis. It was strange not having her around as part of their lives. One night Hannah was checking on the girls, and Alexa was sitting on her bed wearing her best outfit.

"What are you doing, Honey?"

"I'm waiting for Aunt Lori to come and say goodbye. It's okay, Mommy. I hid all my money."

Hannah wanted to cry. She hadn't really understood the full impact that Lori was having on their children.

Lori had been aunt to these children from the day they were born, part of their day-to-day lives. How could they possibly understand why she was no longer around, why they would probably never see her again?

Life resumed without Lori. Her name was brought up less and less in conversation. Things returned to normal. Hannah hired some part-time help, so that she could resume her studies. They spent as many weekends as possible at the lake. Everyone was happy and healthy, until...

Chapter 43

The aphrodisiac, Spanish Fly, is made from the dried
Blister Beetle.

Lori had been incarcerated for well over a year. The
Grahams were living a happy, busy life with little thought
of the past and Lori. Robert had a new assistant, one who
was not intertwined with his personal life. The kids were
busy with sports and artistic endeavors. Hannah was
taking classes online and had resumed training for a
marathon. She ran 10 miles every day. Robert joined her
whenever possible.

Hannah was doing well in her training, getting stronger
every day, but then she started having some health issues,
nothing serious, just feeling weak and having bouts of
mild diarrhea. The stomach issues made it difficult to leave
the house and   she was becoming increasingly
debilitated. At first she wasn't sick enough to go to see Dr.
Lowenstein. The symptoms were annoying more than
anything.

Hannah doubled up on her vitamins and became diligent
about her diet. She felt as if she were in a fog, floating in-
and-out of reality over the following weeks. She had good
days and she had bad days, really bad days. She had lost 20
pounds and was barely able to get out of bed. There had
been several trips to Dr. Lowenstein, numerous tests, but

no answers. Robert became concerned that he was losing her.

The couple hired full-time help at home, for the days that Hannah was unable to do anything. Robert insisted she go to the hospital.

She didn't put up a fight this time, she felt like she wanted to die. The doctors didn't know where to begin with her, so they just started to test her for everything. Each day Hannah became weaker and lost more weight until she finally became comatose. Robert was terrified.

After two weeks in the hospital, the doctors came to pay Robert a visit. "Mr. Graham. We've tried every test that we could think of and we've come up empty handed. We're sorry, but there's nothing more that we can do. You need to start thinking about transition care for your wife." Robert covered his face with both hands and wept. The doctors departed.

Robert sat in the chair next to his wife's bed and cried. He watched Hannah's face for any sign of life…nothing. The nurse came in and handed Robert a box of tissues. "Mr. Graham, I'm here to discuss transition care with you."

"You what?" Robert answered, befuddled.

"Transition care for your wife, morphine to make her comfortable and expedite the process of her passing."

"Nurse, please there must be something that we can do."

"I'm sorry, Mr. Graham, there's nothing more to be done." She suggested that Robert and the children all say their goodbyes to Hannah.

Robert brought the children in to say goodbye to their mother. Just then the new team of doctors arrived from Kansas City to tell Robert the good news...that they had found the source of Hannah's illness: poison. Robert could not fathom who would want to poison Hannah. She had only one enemy and that person was in jail. It made no sense.

"Mr. Graham, we will start your wife on an IV, then our work here is done. Since your wife's body has been poisoned with ricin, it's a federal offense and the FBI will be involved. Good luck to you, sir, finding the person that did this."

"Doctors, I can't thank you enough for saving my wife."

"Before you go, can you tell me please, what is ricin?"

"It's a highly toxic substance made from castor beans. It's frequently used by terrorists, very serious stuff."

Robert nodded, trying to comprehend this new information. "Thank you so much again, doctors."

They all shook hands. The team departed never to be seen by Robert again.

Chapter 44

Ricin can be made from the residue of the processed castor bean.

Ten minutes later, a group of five FBI agents were assembled in Hannah's hospital room. Robert had the children taken home, so he could be alone with the agents. They had many questions for Robert. A new agent in training, Arnie Darrow, was leading the team. He was finishing his training in Alexandria, and his superiors felt that he was more than qualified to take on the case.

Arnie did his best to make Robert feel comfortable. Robert thought Arnie had the looks of a cop, but was too good looking. He had a chiseled face, impeccably spiked salt and pepper hair, twinkling hazel eyes, and dazzling white teeth when he smiled. He had a ruggedness about him, and at the same time was perfectly groomed and his clothes looked expensive.

"Tell me, Mr. Graham, when did your wife first become ill?"

"Please call me Robert. It's been off and on for the past six to eight weeks. It started slowly, then she just went downhill fast."

Arnie made notes as Robert spoke. "We are going to have to search your office, your home, anywhere that Hannah has been lately. We will also be interviewing everyone around her."

"Of course, anything that you need."

"We are going to be very intrusive in your life until we get to the bottom of this. I just want to warn you."

"Do whatever you need to do to find out who did this to my wife."

"You have my word, we will do our best." The two men shook hands. Arnie had enough information from Robert to get started. Hannah would be well enough to speak for herself in a few days.

"One more thing before I go. You may want to get your children out of the house for a while. It can be disturbing to watch us go through all of your possessions."

"Yes, of course. I'll arrange to have them stay with Hannah's mom." Robert gave Arnie keys to his office, the house in Arlington and the lake house before the detective left.

Darrow started with the office. His team of five arrived and they proceeded to tear the place apart. It took three days. They made notes as they worked. The fourth day, they were combing through the Graham house.

Arnie received a call that Hannah was feeling well enough to talk to him. Darrow dropped everything and went directly to Hannah's hospital room.

Hannah was sitting up in bed when Darrow arrived. She looked tiny and pale, but she had an enormous smile on her face when Arnie entered the room. "Hello, Mrs. Graham, I'm Investigator Darrow from the FBI. It's such a pleasure to meet you and to see that you are doing so well." He extended his hand to Hannah.

"Thank you, but please just call me Hannah."

"Okay, Hannah, and you can call me Arnie."

"Thank you Arnie, for helping us find out who did this to me."

"I have a lot of questions for you Hannah. Are you ready?"

"Shoot." she said.

Hannah studied his face as he spoke. He was definitely a man's man, she thought, and kind of rough and rugged. It didn't look to her like he had a woman in his life to take care of him. Too bad, she thought, he looked like he could use some attention and care from a woman. She managed to focus her thoughts on his questions.

"I need to know everything Hannah, over the past two months, where you've been, who you've been in contact with, everything. I'll need a list of your friends, family, and a detailed accounting of your day-to-day life, every little detail, everything. Arnie made notes as she talked.

"What about this Lori person?"

"Yes, she most definitely would want to poison me, but she's in prison. Pretty good alibi I would say."

She told him the entire story from the time she met Lori in college.

"Wow, that's quite a story. She sounds like a piece of work. You're right, prison is a pretty airtight alibi, but I still need to check out every lead." Hannah told him all about Josh and the boys, giving him a list of their full names and contact information.

Hannah had been talking incessantly for an hour and was getting tired. "I'm sorry Arnie, is it okay if we continue this tomorrow? I'm pretty worn out."

"Absolutely, you get some rest." Arnie headed back to the Graham house. He was waiting for Robert when he got home from work.

"Hi Arnie, I'm surprised to see you're still here. What's up? Any leads yet?"

"Several actually. I wanted to ask you something."

"Sure, go ahead."

"What is this about?" He handed the nude photo of Robert and Lori to him. "That's sort of a strange thing to keep around the house. Weren't you afraid that your wife would see it?"

Robert half grinned, "Well, Arnie, that's a really weird story. Would you like to join me in a beer and hear all about it?"

"Sure, sounds intriguing."

Robert pulled out a couple of Red Stripes and the two took a seat at the kitchen table. Robert told the whole story and it sounded believable to him as he was saying it. "Pretty weird, wouldn't you say?"

"Very."

"Oh, yeah, and Hannah knows all about it, everything. You can ask her."

"You have a pretty understanding wife Robert."

"Very."

Chapter 45

Ricin can be inactivated in heat over 80 degrees.

Arnie decided that it was time to pay a visit to Lori. The next morning he made the two plus hour drive to Troy where she was incarcerated. She was nothing like what Arnie had expected, and she looked nothing like the photo that he had of her. He expected a chubby brunette, what he found was a skinny woman, with short, spiky ash blond hair.

"Thank you for talking to me today." Arnie started the conversation.

"My pleasure." Lori was turning on the charm. "You're awfully good looking to be an FBI agent."

"Thanks, I guess." Arnie was embarrassed and annoyed. He was there to find answers, not to be flattered.

"So tell me Investigator Darrow, what is it that I can help you with today?"

"I'm here about Hannah. Someone has been poisoning her."

"Oh, I heard about that. You certainly don't think I had anything to do with that do you?"

"No, not really, you have a pretty tight alibi. I just wanted to talk to you. Maybe you can tell me something about Hannah that I don't know."

"I can tell you a lot about that little princess. She thinks that her shit doesn't stink if you know what I mean. Everyone thinks Hannah is so wonderful and so perfect. God, how I used to get sick of hearing that! What's so great about her anyway? She has my life. Those should have been my kids, Robert should be my husband, and all of that money should be mine! She took my life. I hate that little bitch!"

"I had no idea that you felt that way. Why should it all be yours?"

"Because I dated Robert first. It was my life until she stepped in. She ruined everything.

"Sounds like you really have it in for her."

"I do. Hate the bitch and everything about her."

"Would you want to cause her harm?"

"Absolutely, but it's kind of difficult to cause anyone harm from in here."

"What can you tell me about Josh and the boys?"

"I can tell you that I hate Josh almost as much as I hate Hannah. He's the reason that I'm in here, he and his big mouth. The rest of the boys are all pretty harmless."

"Can you think of anyone that might want to hurt Hannah?"

"I don't know why anyone wouldn't want to harm the bitch, if you know what I mean."

"Thanks you for your time, Lori. You've been a real help."

"That's it? That's all you have to ask me? I've got lots of stories to tell about Hannah. Come on sit down and stay for a while."

"Thank you anyway, Lori. I've got to go now." Arnie couldn't wait to get away from her. Lori was livid that she wasn't given more time to be the center of his investigation. She loved the attention.

Arnie stopped to talk to a couple of the guards on his way out. He showed them an old picture of Lori. "Can you tell me what happened to her?" He pointed to Lori. "She used to look like this, and now she looks like that."

The two guards looked at one another and laughed. "That happens a lot in here. They lose a drastic amount of weight, fast. The food is really bad."

"What about the hair, the whole look?"

"That's because she lives in the 'butch' wing."

"The butch wing? What is that?"

"She's a lesbian and they are kept separate from the straight ones. Just makes life a whole lot easier around here." Arnie was perplexed. He had had no idea that Lori was a lesbian.

Arnie decided to stop by the hospital to talk to Hannah before calling it a day. Hannah was looking much stronger.

She was visibly happy to see Arnie. "What a nice surprise, Arnie! I get to go home tomorrow."

"That's wonderful news Hannah."

"What's going on with the investigation? Have you found any leads yet?"

"I'm working on a few different theories. Why didn't you ever mention that Lori was a lesbian?"

"A lesbian? Are you sure? I had no idea!"

"Me neither; something is weird. I need to do some more digging."

"I'm going to pay a visit to some of the boys tomorrow."

"Please give them my best, would you?"

"Of course. It's been a long day. Hannah, you take care of yourself and I'll talk to you soon."

"Thanks, Arnie. Take care."

Arnie didn't want to tell Hannah that he had been to see Lori or how much that she despised Hannah. She had to use all of her strength now just to get better.

Arnie had scheduled back-to-back interviews with the boys at the Majestic on King Street. All of the boys were obviously enamored with Hannah and tired of Lori and her antics. The interviews all went smoothly and swiftly, except for the interview with Josh. He had much to tell Arnie and it was rather disturbing.

Josh had been privy to Lori's innermost thoughts for many years. She was not a happy or a healthy person. She portrayed herself as a kind and caring person to others, but internally she was something entirely different. Holding on to her painful childhood, she was consumed with rage, resentment and jealousy.

Josh filled Arnie in on the notes that he had sent to Hannah and Robert over the years, and his infamous lunch with Hannah where he dropped the bomb about the embezzling.

"The Grahams are the most wonderful people. I hated to see what Lori was doing to them. In the beginning she was fun to be around, then it just got old watching her be so hateful and vindictive all of the time."

"Did you know that she is a lesbian?" Arnie asked.

"A lesbian? Ha! She will do or be anything that suits her needs. I'm sure that she is only a lesbian because she is in prison and somehow she can get something out of it. No, I don't believe that she is really a lesbian."

Arnie thought Josh's answer was most interesting. The two men talked for a couple of hours. "Thank you for your time and for being so candid."

"I've always felt guilty that I never said anything sooner. Poor Hannah has been through so much because of that witch."

"Before I go, I thought you might like to see what Lori looks like today." He showed Josh a recent photo of Lori.

"What do you know? Wow, a skinny butch. Go figure. She sure has the look down!" The two men shook hands and parted.

Chapter 46

Ricin prevents the body from producing the proteins that it needs in order to survive.

Hannah was finally well enough to go home. Her mother came to stay and help with the kids for a few weeks until Hannah was fully recovered. She was thrilled to be home and well. Everyone was not only happy to have her home, but to have her alive! No one was taking anything for granted.

The investigation continued. Arnie's team had been working diligently on going through the lake house, interviewing Hannah's friends and family, anything that they could think of. The ricin had been ingested, so they had to focus on that. Who would have had the opportunity to slip the poison to Hannah through food on a regular basis? They meticulously followed every possible lead.

Three weeks into the investigation Arnie requested a meeting with Hannah and Robert, alone. They met in Robert's office.

"I just want you two to know what is happening. There will be an arrest made tomorrow. We've found the person who did this to Hannah."

"Oh, my god! Who is it, Arnie?" Hannah's heart was pounding. She knew that whoever it was, it wasn't going to be good.

"Her name is Michelle Tompkins." Robert and Hannah gave one another a quizzical look.

"Who?" They asked in unison. "Are we supposed to know her?" Hannah asked.

"No, Hannah, you don't know her by name, but you do know her face. Let me explain." Robert and Hannah watched Arnie intently waiting for his story.

"There were a few things that led me to Michelle Tompkins. The most important thing was opportunity. She had the opportunity to poison Hannah on a regular basis."

"But, I don't even know who she is!"

"I'm getting there. Just give me a minute. True, she did not appear to have a motive, but indirectly she did."

"What? I'm not following," Hannah stated.

The person with the most obvious motive was Lori, but she didn't have the opportunity. Michelle had the opportunity, but seemingly no motive. When you put the two women together it ties the whole thing in."

"But how?"

"They were roommates and lovers in Troy."

"Are you shitting me?" Robert exclaimed.

"That is just bizarre." Hannah added.

"So who is this Michelle person and how was she able to poison me regularly?"

"She's your local barista. You stop and have one of her lattes every day after your run."

"Oh my god! This is crazy."

"Michelle was on early release. She was carrying out Lori's wishes. Lori pretended to be in love with Michelle so that she would do this for her, knowing that she could never be caught for it." Robert and Hannah listened silently with their jaws dropped.

"Wait, there's more." Arnie continued.

"Josh said something that really stuck in my mind. He had remembered seeing homegrown beans in Lori's apartment once and asked her about them. She said that she was trying to eat organically. Well, that's just bullshit. Lori has never eaten anything organic in her life. I believe she was growing castor beans for ricin way back then.

Robert, I looked through your medical records and it all fits. She was giving you the same poison all those years ago that she was giving to Hannah."

"This is all so insane." Hannah chimed in.

"Yes, precisely. The woman is diabolical, pathological."

Robert interrupted, "So we know that she hated Hannah and that's why she was having her poisoned, but why me all of those years ago?"

"She was in your will then. You were worth more to her dead than alive. She first started to poison you just a little, to keep you and Hannah from seeing one another. Later on she became much more serious about it. She really tried hard to kill you once she found out about you and Hannah being married.

The first wedding in Fiji wasn't a legal wedding in this country. If she had killed you before the third marriage, she would have inherited everything. Hannah wouldn't have gotten a thing. I looked at the timing in your medical records and it all adds up. When she failed at the poisoning, she took the nude photos as insurance in case you had decided to cut her out of your will."

"Good god, and to think that we used to trust that woman with our children!" Robert exclaimed.

"This all sounds like a bad movie." Hannah added.

"So now what do we do? She gets out soon." Robert asked.

"She will be prosecuted for your poisoning, Robert. The statute of limitations is not over yet. Don't worry, it will be a cold day in hell before she gets out, and Michelle will be put away as well."

"Arnie, we can never thank you enough." Robert shook his hand. "Just doing my job. Glad I could help. You two have a wonderful evening. Go out and celebrate the fact that this is all over and that now you can lead normal lives."

The couple took Arnie's advice. They brought home a bottle of champagne and opened it as they filled Hannah's mom in on everything. They also brought home pizza for the kids. Amy listened, wide-eyed, as they described the details of the day.

Chapter 47

Ricin is in the same deadly weapon class as anthrax.

The following evening there was a knock at the front door. Robert answered. It was Arnie Darrow. "Arnie, I didn't expect to see you again so soon."

"Oh, I'm not here to see you, I'm here to pick up Amy for dinner."

"Amy? Really?" Robert chuckled. "Come on in, I'll get her for you." Hannah offered him a glass of wine while he waited. She tried her best not to look surprised.

Amy appeared looking like an older version of her daughter. She was neatly dressed in a pair of black silk pants, black sandals and a white blouse. She finished the look with a multi strand white baroque pearl necklace. Her dark blond hair had been recently trimmed to chin length. Arnie was obviously pleased with what he saw. The two did not hang around for a glass of wine. They were out the door right away.

Hannah and Robert exchanged glances the moment they were gone. Both erupted in laughter at the same time. "Did you know about this?" Hannah asked.

"I had no idea."

"Who would have ever guessed that those two would get together? I never really thought about my mom dating, but she has been widowed for a very long time."

"Go figure."

Arnie commented to Amy, "You look very beautiful tonight."

"Thank you. You don't look so bad yourself." Amy found Arnie to be extremely handsome, very polished. He was wearing a pair of black pants, black loafers, a gray cashmere sweater and he smelled wonderful. Amy got a whiff of his cologne as he opened the door to his BMW Z4 for her. "You smell great." She commented.

"Thanks," He responded with a huge grin.

They arrived at La Lucia in Old Town and were quickly escorted to a quiet booth. "Do you like wine, Amy?"

"Yes, of course."

"Anything in particular?"

"No, not really." Arnie ordered a bottle of Virginia Meritage.

"So, Amy, tell me about yourself."

Amy gave him a brief synopsis of her life and how her life had suddenly changed when her husband, Charles, died. "I know how that happens all too well, when my wife Noelle died, everything changed."

"I'm sorry, Arnie. I didn't realize that you had lost your wife."

"It's been a few years now, breast cancer."

"Please tell me about Noelle. Where did you two meet? How long were you married?"

He opened up to Amy about his life and about losing Noelle, and feeling lost.

"We met as freshmen, we were both attending Harvard."

"You went to Harvard? That's most unusual for a cop!" I suppose so. At the time I was studying literature."

"Really, Arnie? What in the world happened that you went from literature to law?"

"Noelle became pregnant so I had to quit school and find something to pay the bills. Being a cop sounded interesting to me. I liked the idea of rescuing people. Call me a romantic."

"Arnie you are just full of surprises!"

"We had a wonderful life together. Noelle was very quiet, sweet and of course exotic, being from Paris. We adored one another and were happy with the arrival of our daughter Anna."

"Where is Anna now?"

"She's finishing her senior year at Wellesley. I really am not comfortable talking about myself so much. It's just that life changed drastically when Noelle died. I became a real mess. It wasn't until working on the Kenneth Alexander case that I became focused and decided to become an FBI agent. I was sloppy, disheveled, and unkempt. Some friends took pity on me when we were vacationing in Tahoe. They got me cleaned up, new haircut, and clothes shopping, etc. They really came to my rescue."

"It looks like they did a great job, Arnie. You look wonderful."

"Things are pretty good for me right now."

"I didn't realize that we had so much in common, both being widowed and all."

"No, I didn't either. Small world I guess."

"You already know quite a bit about me from the investigation, I'd like to know a little more about you. What is your daughter studying?"

"Believe it or not, she wants to follow in my footsteps. She wants to be involved with law somehow so we'll see."

"What about your wife, what did she do?"

"She was a musician, a very talented musician."

The two chatted on through the rest of the evening, having much to talk about. Arnie took Amy back to the Graham house and asked if he could see her again. Amy was pleased by the invitation.

She gave Arnie a kiss on the cheek, and said, "You still smell good." Arnie just smiled.

Chapter 48

One gram of purified ricin can kill about 36,000 people.

Life was returning to normal in the Graham house. The children would occasionally ask questions about Lori. Why did she never come to visit? Why did she never say goodbye? Why did she take their money? They did their best to explain it to the children, but how could they possibly be expected to understand?

Life was happy and carefree, no more worries about anything bad looming in the background. The children were growing up healthy and fast. They spent as much time as possible at the lake. It was October when Robert handed an envelope to Hannah one night after dinner. "What's this?"

"An early Christmas present. Just open it."

Hannah had learned not to like surprises anymore, but she was game. Inside were six airline tickets to Nadi. "I don't understand."

"We are taking the whole family to Turtle Island for Christmas. We are celebrating life!"

Hannah dropped the envelope and threw her arms around Robert's neck. "Thank you so much, Robert. This is such a wonderful surprise. I just can't believe it!"

The Graham family had a layover in Auckland before continuing to Nadi. They checked in to the Hilton and slept until the following afternoon. Hannah had made dinner reservations at the Harbourside Seafood Bar and Grill. When they arrived there were eight people seated at their massive table: Jack, his wife and six children. It was quite a reunion. Hannah had never seen Jack look so relaxed and happy. Being married to a native Fijian suited him and being father of six was agreeing with him.

The two had stayed in touch over the years and it was finally good to see one another. The children and spouses all got along famously. It was a wonderful, festive evening and all were sad to have it end. The two families said their goodbyes promising to continue to stay in touch.

The next morning they flew to Nadi and connected to a flight to Turtle Island. There was Mike, bare feet and all. He recognized Hannah instantly. The two had much to talk about on the short ride. The family of six barely fit into Mike's small seaplane. The entire island showed up to greet the plane.

Most of the staff was the same as was there for Hannah and Robert's honeymoon. It was incredible to see everyone again. It is a rare occasion that anyone returns to Turtle Island, especially with children in tow.

The children had a wonderful time fishing, riding horses and frolicking in the ocean. The staff had special events planned for the children, teaching them native Fijian crafts and singing native songs. Hannah especially loved taking the children horseback riding around the island every morning.

Robert had planned a special day ahead of time. The staff loaded the Graham family into two of their small-motorized boats and headed off to Hannah's Moturiki Island. Hannah's host family had prepared a large brunch that was waiting for them. There was much catching up to do.

After brunch everyone was loaded back into the boats, this time to pay a visit to the medicine man. Tears came to his eyes the moment he saw Hannah. He treated the family to a kava ceremony. Robert explained everything to the children as the ceremony transpired.

The visit was over way too fast, and it was back to the Moturiki Island. When they returned, Samu was waiting on the beach with six saddled horses. Hannah threw her arms around Samu's neck.

"Oh, how I've missed you and our rides!"

The two had corresponded occasionally over the years. They exchanged letters and Hannah sometimes sent items that Samu had requested that he couldn't buy in Fiji.

Samu led the way with the Graham family in tow. Little Ginny shared a horse with her mom. Hannah took in the beauty of the island. She was so grateful to be back in this breathtaking place that she loved so much and how wonderful it was to be sharing it with her family!

The "Hannah" gold baroque freshwater pearl necklace is available on SaylorStorm.com for purchase